Praise for Marie Ferrarella:

"Ferrarella has penned a guaranteed page-turner!"
—*Romantic Times* on *Internal Affair*

"Time and again, Marie Ferrarella demonstrates her
gift for storytelling in the romantic suspense genre,
and *Crime and Passion* is no exception."
—*Romantic Times* on *Crime and Passion*

"…the saucy quips will draw a laugh,
and the chemistry will make you shiver.
Marie Ferrarella does it again!"
—*Romantic Times* on *Mac's Bedside Manner*

"Great romance, excellent plot,
grabs you from page one."
—*Affaire de Coeur* on *In Graywolf's Hands*

"…the pleasure of this journey is in the getting
there. Reading about warm, caring people and
watching relationships mature under stressful
situations is a pleasurable way to spend an
afternoon. As usual, Ferrarella's dialogue is in voice,
crisp, and moves the story along without ever
bogging down in the emotional angst each brings to
the relationship. *Once a Father* is a hearty
recommend for a skilled writer."
—*The Romance Reader* on *Once a Father*

THE FORTUNES OF TEXAS:
Reunion

MARIE FERRARELLA
A Baby Changes Everything

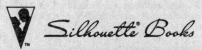
Silhouette Books

Published by Silhouette Books

America's Publisher of Contemporary Romance

Special thanks and acknowledgment are given
to Marie Ferrarella for her contribution
to THE FORTUNES OF TEXAS: REUNION series.

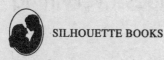

SILHOUETTE BOOKS

A BABY CHANGES EVERYTHING

Copyright © 2005 by Harlequin Books S.A.

ISBN 0-373-38927-2

Visit Silhouette Books at www.eHarlequin.com

Printed in U.S.A.

Dear Reader,

It isn't often that we get a chance to see if happily ever after is all it's cracked up to be. When I was invited to do the second book in THE FORTUNES OF TEXAS: REUNION continuity, I discovered that I was being reunited with two characters I had brought together in *Expecting in Texas* and they were having problems. Although they still loved each other as much as ever, life and reality had found a way to put a wedge between them. Cruz worked too hard to create the kind of life he felt his family deserved and Savannah felt as if she was being taken for granted. (Sound familiar? Yeah, me, too.) Juggling as fast as they could, they had no energy left to devote to the marriage they had created. And let's face it, marriage takes work. Constant work. Changes were going to have to be made. But I'm betting that Savannah and Cruz are up to it. How about you?

I wish you love,

Marie Ferrarella

To Stella Bagwell, who no longer has a brain,
because I've picked it clean.
Many thanks, Stella, for all your help.

One

"Hey, I'd given up on you two."

Vanessa Fortune Kincaid threw open the door on the first ring and immediately hugged her dearest friend in the world as the latter began to cross the threshold. Stepping back, Vanessa took a closer look at Savannah Perez and decided that she didn't like what she saw. Savannah's bright, sunny smile was conspicuously absent.

Ushering her five-year-old son, Luke, in front of her, Savannah sighed. Luke hadn't stopped talking or moving since he'd opened his eyes this morning. The word *lively,* she had come to believe, had been created expressly to describe her son.

Savannah forced her lips into a weak smile. It was the best she could offer her friend. "You wouldn't be the first one."

Vanessa had dropped down to one knee to give her godson a huge embrace. The boy smelled faintly of raspberry jam and peanut butter, his sandwich of choice. "How's the handsomest man in three states?"

Luke beamed. "Fine, Aunt 'Nessa."

He shoved his hands into the back pockets of his jeans, just like his father, and cocked his head, his dark eyes huge as he asked, "Got something for me?"

"Luke!" Embarrassment brought the only visible color to Savannah's pale cheeks. "You don't ask someone to give you a present."

"I'm not 'someone,'" Vanessa said, winking at the boy. "I'm Aunt 'Nessa." Rising to her feet, Vanessa waved her hand at Savannah's protest. They'd been friends far too long to leave any room for embarrassment over imagined neglected niceties.

Vanessa walked to a credenza and opened one small door. "And, as a matter of fact, I do have something for Luke."

Taking out an object, she tucked it behind her back as she turned to face the boy.

Luke was dancing from one foot to the other, his dark eyes shining.

With a pleasure-filled laugh, Vanessa handed her godson the very latest in action figures. The buffed character breaking out of his painted-on shirt was from a new movie that was yet to be released but was already a hit among the under-twelve set.

Luke gave a loud whoop of joy. "Wow, it's Big Jake, the monster killer."

"And he even comes with his own monster to kill." Vanessa pointed to a lesser figure that was included, easily overshadowed by the hero.

"Wow," Luke echoed. He tugged at the packaging, eager to get at his prize. Vanessa helped him. Freed of their plastic prison, the two figures popped up into the air.

Savannah shook her head. "You're spoiling him, Vanessa."

Luke sat down and was soon happily immersed in a fantasy reenactment of a battle royal between the hero and the monster, apparently oblivious to his mother and her friend.

Watching him, Vanessa smiled broadly. "Hey, I like roaming through toy stores. Shopping for Luke gives me an excuse to be there." After her miscarriage, she wanted a baby more than ever. Now that her husband, Devin's, desk job at the FBI only took him away occasionally, there was a better chance to make that happen.

She ruffled the boy's jet-black hair, then walked over to Savannah, taking a seat beside her on the wide, cream-colored leather sofa. Savannah was huddled to one side, leaning against the upholstered arm as if she intended to use it to help keep her up.

Concern flitted through Vanessa as she sat down. Savannah hadn't sounded quite like herself on the telephone when she'd asked to come over.

Seeing her didn't alter that impression.

Vanessa grew serious. "What did you mean when you said I wouldn't be the first?"

Savannah looked from her son to her friend. "What?"

Vanessa had a pitcher of iced tea standing at the ready on a tray on the coffee table. Without bothering to extend an invitation, she poured a tall glass for Savannah and one for herself. Two bottles of chilled soda waited on Luke's pleasure.

"When you walked in," she reminded Savannah, hand-ing her a glass. "I said I'd given up on you two, and you said I wouldn't be the first. What did you mean by that?"

Wrapping her hands around the glass, Savannah shrugged carelessly. It was a subject she'd just as soon dismiss. But she knew better. Vanessa had a way of hanging on to something once she'd gotten her teeth into it.

Savannah took a long sip of the cool liquid before offering a vague answer. "Just me, feeling sorry for myself, that's all."

Vanessa gave her a long, penetrating look. This wasn't just a passing mood, she thought. This was something more. Was there trouble on Paradise Island? "Want to talk about it?"

Savannah stared at the amber liquid. In the background, Luke's monster gave a bloodcurdling yell as Jake killed him. "No."

Vanessa glanced in Luke's direction to make sure everything was all right. The boy had started a new scenario. She looked back at Savannah.

"Yes, you do," Vanessa said firmly. Savannah began to protest, but the words never left her mouth, halted by Vanessa's knowing look. "You wouldn't be here if you didn't. You know I won't leave it alone until you tell me. When you walk in here—" she gestured around the house with her free hand "—or anywhere near me, you do *not* have the right to remain silent." She leaned closer, lowering her voice even though she doubted that Luke could hear. He was too busy being Jake and the monster. "Now, what's wrong?"

Feeling empty, weary beyond her years and lonelier than she could remember being in a very long time, Savannah murmured, "It's nothing." She stared again at her tall, frosted glass, noting the tiny rivulets of water had begun to run along the sides.

Like tears, Savannah thought. *Just like my tears.*

Vanessa frowned. " 'Nothing' wouldn't have you looking like a wilted flower." Her eyes swept over her friend's form. Five months pregnant and barely a discernible clue from her body. How did she do it? "You're supposed to be glowing by now."

Glowing, ha. Most mornings Savannah felt like ashes from a day-old campfire. With a shake of her head, she laughed dryly. "Whoever made that assessment of motherhood was obviously a man. On my best day, I don't 'glow.' I manage."

And just barely, she added silently. Between doing the bookkeeping for the ranch, handling Luke, morning sickness and the housekeeping, she was coming perilously close to losing it on all fronts. The faster she juggled, the more certain she was that she was going to drop something. Or everything.

But in her heart she knew that if she just had a little support, she could do it.

She might as well be wishing for the moon, she thought sadly.

Savannah could feel her friend studying her. Vanessa always seemed to know just what she was thinking. Now was no exception.

"But it's not just the pregnancy getting you down, is it?" she asked.

"No, it's not." Taking another sip of her iced tea, Savannah put the glass back on the tray. "You know, the police force could use your clairvoyance. You're going to waste here."

Vanessa put her hand on top of Savannah's, forcing her

friend to look at her instead of avoiding her eyes. "Stop trying to change the subject. Tell me what's wrong."

Savannah knotted her fingers together in her lap, staring down at them.

"Everything," she finally whispered, so quietly that, even sitting next to her, Vanessa had to strain to hear.

Tears suddenly filled Savannah's eyes, spilling out. Annoyed, she wiped them away with the back of her hand. "Damn, I still haven't gotten the hang of riding this emotional roller coaster. You'd think that the second time around would be easier, not harder." She sighed, feeling as if everything was conspiring against her. But she knew that if only Cruz would love her the way he used to, everything else would fall into place. "There should be a way to put your hormones in cold storage for the duration, get them back after you push out the baby."

Feeling for her, Vanessa put her arm around Savannah's small shoulders. "Have you told Cruz what you're going through?"

Savannah drew back and laughed. The sound had no pleasure in it.

"Cruz?" He was the whole problem, not a solution. Although if he'd only change again... "I'd have to make an appointment to talk to him. And even then he'd probably only break it or, worse, forget to show up altogether."

Vanessa was very quiet for a moment. There was something in Savannah's face that had her heart freezing. She tried to read between the lines and hoped fervently that she was wrong. "My God, there's isn't another woman, is there?"

Another woman, Savannah thought. If only...

"Well," she said slowly, "yes, in a manner of speaking there is another woman."

There might as well have been, for all the time Cruz spent away from the house, Savannah thought. A slight trace of bitterness entered her voice. Who would have thought that the promise of success would do this to them? Money had never meant anything to her. Only love and Cruz had.

"He spends almost all his time with her." Savannah laughed shortly, recalling the last few months, so awful in their loneliness. "By the time I get him back, he can hardly make conversation, much less act like the man who made my head spin and my pulse race."

Vanessa curled her fingers into her palms, trying to curb the desire to beat on Cruz even though she'd grown up liking him. Until he'd married Savannah, Cruz had worked on her father's ranch, the Double Crown. She and her brothers and sister had grown up playing with Cruz and his sisters, calling him friend.

Now she was calling him something a whole lot less flattering in her mind.

"Well, who is she?" Vanessa demanded. "Have you tried confronting her?" She put herself in Savannah's shoes. "I know if there was some woman who was trying to get her hooks into Devin, I'd knock her into next Tuesday." She looked at Savannah, suddenly mindful of her condition. It was so hard to remember she was pregnant, given what Savannah looked like. "I could do that for you, you know. You're pregnant, you don't want to get yourself upset. But I could certainly handle this bitch for you. What's her name?"

"La Esperanza." Hope, that was what he'd named it. Hope, because that was what it represented to both of them. Hope for a new start, hope for the future. And now it had taken all hope away from her.

Vanessa stared at her. "The ranch?" she asked incredulously.

"The ranch," Savannah confirmed. "Cruz refers to our ranch as 'she.'" The more she thought about it, the more fitting it seemed. "And La Esperanza is a hell of a lot more competition than any flesh-and-blood woman I ever knew."

At least, if it had been another woman, she'd like to think she'd know how to compete. But the ranch had been her husband's dream ever since she could remember. How could she possibly compete against a dream?

"But he's just doing that for his family. For you," Vanessa argued.

No, not for her, Savannah thought. Because if it was for her, he would have stopped knocking himself out a long time ago. He would have tried to fit her into his day, into his night, instead of living and breathing work on the ranch.

"He's doing that for himself," Savannah said firmly. Ever loyal to the man she loved with all her heart, she softened slightly, as if she couldn't help but take his side, at least to a minor degree. "Oh, he wants to be a good provider and all, but part of being a good provider is being there in more than just body. And he's not." She sighed, looking past her friend, focusing instead on the last few months. Maybe even years, she amended. This had been going on and steadily getting worse for a long, long time. "He hasn't been for a long while now."

Trying to lighten the moment and do away with the dark look in her friend's eyes, Vanessa patted Savannah's stomach. "Well, he must have been there in body and spirit at least once."

Savannah shook her head. "I need more than just once.

I need more than just a part-time husband, although at this point I'd settle for that. What I have is a husband who's there ten percent of the time. And usually that ten percent is spent in bed."

"Quality, not quantity, has always been my motto."

"Sleeping," Savannah emphasized. "And although he looks really cute that way…" She looked toward her son, who had once more dropped down onto the rug. Jake was smashing in the monster's face. "A little like Luke, really. But it's hard to maintain a two-way conversation with a man who's doing a fairly good imitation of a corpse."

Savannah took in a deep breath, knowing that she was coming very close to crying again. That wasn't why she'd come here. She didn't want to cry; she wanted to forget about everything for a little while.

"Cruz is up and out of the house before sunrise, back after sunset—sometimes long after sunset." Sadness twisted her soul. "I have to show Luke pictures of the man just to remind him what his father looks like."

Vanessa shook her head as she laughed. "C'mon now, you're exaggerating."

Savannah sighed. There was sadness in her eyes as she looked up at her best friend. "Not as much as I wish I was."

Communication was the only way, Vanessa thought. It certainly worked for her and Devin. "Have you told him how you feel?"

Savannah looked at her. Hadn't she been listening? "I just said—"

"I know what you just said," Vanessa interrupted, squelching a minor bout of impatience. The solution, or at least a start, seemed pretty clear to her. "That you'd have to make an appointment to see him. Well, make one. Do whatever it takes. Grab him by the arm when he walks in tonight and say, 'Cruz, we have to talk.'" She waved her hand, as if trying to bring about a magic spell. "And then talk."

"He'll probably fall asleep while I'm talking."

Cruz had done that just the other night. Right after dinner. He hadn't even got up from the table. He'd laid his head down for a second, just to "rest my eyes," and boom, he was out like a light. It took everything she had not to put on the radio and blast him. But she hadn't. She'd gently prodded him to his feet and then, with his arm slung across her shoulders, she'd somehow managed to get him up the stairs and into bed. During the one occasion when he'd been intoxicated and the same thing had happened, he'd pulled her down on top of him and they'd made love.

This time, though, he'd gone straight back to sleep.

Leaving her out in the cold.

"It won't be the first time," Savannah concluded, keeping her voice low for Luke's sake. It throbbed with emotion.

Vanessa glanced at the iced tea container. "Then keep a pitcher of cold water handy and douse him if you have to."

Despite the situation, Savannah heard herself laughing. "You're a radical woman, Vanessa Kincaid, you know that?"

Vanessa winked in response. "Maybe, but I get results."

He had begun to think that today was never going to be over. Since before sunup, the day had felt endless.

Which, he supposed, made it no different from all the others that had come before it in the last few months. His days were stretched to the maximum, filled from beginning to end with work. By the time he finally walked up to the house each evening, Cruz Perez felt as if he barely had enough energy to put one foot in front of the other.

Certainly not enough to sit and talk the way Savannah always wanted to do when he walked in through the front door.

He wished he had the energy she required of him.

He wished she could understand.

Getting the life he wanted for them required a great deal of sacrifice on his part. And part of that sacrifice meant not doing what he would rather be doing.

Which was being with Savannah.

He loved his wife. He really did, he thought as he drove up the winding lane to his house. Loved her with every fiber of his being.

But at the same time, the very sight of Savannah made him acutely aware of all his shortcomings. They came at him from all directions, illuminated with glaring headlights. They made him ashamed, because he couldn't give her what he wanted to give her.

A woman like Savannah deserved to have things, things he couldn't find a way to give her no matter how hard he tried. How hard he worked.

He always knew that running a ranch wouldn't be easy, but he had lusted after it as far back as he could remember. Having a ranch made you your own man, gave you something to make you proud.

If it was successful.

Lately, though, there were more headaches, more bills than there was joy. A lot more.

And then there was the new baby coming—a baby that hadn't been planned.

Lightning certainly did strike twice, he thought, driving his Jeep into the garage. Getting out, he began to walk toward the house. Luke had certainly not been planned. His firstborn had been the result of a night of passion, the kind that most men only dreamed about.

Cruz's mouth curved as he remembered. He'd been working for the Fortunes then, with a chip on his shoulder and an army of women trailing after him. He'd had more than his share, but from the first moment he laid eyes on her, he'd seen something special about the quiet beauty who was Vanessa Fortune's friend.

Savannah was genteel, refined, not like the other women he'd bedded. Women who wanted a wild ride with the rebel stallion, who hadn't seen him for who he really was. Savannah had looked into his eyes, and he'd felt that she was seeing things inside of him that he had only been wishing were there.

She made him want to be a better man.

Still, when she'd left soon afterward, he'd locked her memory away and gone on with his work, being a horse whisperer. Gone on with his life, bedding every willing woman he came across. But even then, Savannah had haunted the perimeters of his mind, making him long for her even though she was an unattainable dream.

After she'd lost her teaching position in a prim and proper private school, she'd returned, to work for the Fortunes as the Double Crown's bookkeeper. He'd been stunned to see her belly slightly rounded with child. *His* child, although pride had her denying it at first.

Pride was the one thing they had in common. Her pride wouldn't let him marry her out of a sense of obligation, so she'd lied to him about the baby's father. And his pride wouldn't allow Savannah to be married to anyone but a success.

It still didn't.

He was determined to be that success for her. And for his son. Honor demanded nothing less.

He'd expanded on the original ranch's one hundred acres, buying more land to the east, planning on having more horses, planning to put the name of La Esperanza on the map. This ranch would never rival in size anything the Fortunes had, but in quality...well, that he could strive for. That would be something worthy he could give Savannah and Luke and whoever else was joining the family in six months. No, four, he mentally corrected himself after ticking off the months in his mind.

Damn, it was hard to keep that straight. Hard to keep anything in his life straight these days, what with one thing after another. Just the day-to-day chores were overwhelming now that Paco had left for reasons that had nothing to do with Cruz.

Didn't matter what the reasons, he thought, walking up to the front door. He still felt the man's loss. Paco had been with him since the beginning and had remained more out of loyalty than the pay. Cruz was down to three hands. The money he'd set aside to hire a new man had been eaten up by vet bills when one of his mares had been bitten by a rattlesnake. He'd come close to having to put her down, but now she was out of the woods. And he was very close to being out of money.

That left him a man short, with him having to take up the slack, since in clear conscience he couldn't ask anyone else to do it. He wasn't that kind of a boss, wanting his hands to do more than he did himself.

It was after nine. The last bit of July daylight had been siphoned off, and night had descended, sitting oppressively over the terrain along with its humidity.

He felt more dead than alive, but he remembered to stomp his boots on the doormat with its faded Welcome sign. He knew how Savannah hated having dirt tracked into the house.

Lately, there seemed to be a lot of things Savannah hated, he thought.

He followed the trail of lights, shutting them off as he went. Electric bills didn't pay for themselves.

He found her sitting at the table in the small dining room. She turned her face toward him as he entered. The table was set for two.

A sad smile twisted his lips. Savannah had given up setting it for three. Luke had long since gone to bed.

Cruz missed his son. Missed his wife. Missed enjoying his life. But sitting back and enjoying things was for dreamers. Not for men with responsibilities.

Someday, he promised himself, he would be able to kick back a little and enjoy the fruit of his labors, like the Fortune men he'd grown up with. Right now was his time to prosper.

But only if he kept after it.

He leaned over and kissed the top of her head. "Hi," he said wearily.

Savannah forced a smile to her lips. He looked as tired as she felt, she thought. "You made it home," she murmured.

His broad shoulders moved in a careless shrug beneath a faded denim work shirt that was damp with sweat. "I always do."

He said that as if he resented coming home to her, she thought. She took a breath. "Hungry?"

Yes, he was hungry. Hungry for a lot of things. Hungry for more than food. But all his body begged for was some place to drop so that it could finally, finally rest. Cruz shook his head.

"No, I'll just turn in."

She looked at the food, which had long since cooled, waiting on his arrival. After leaving Vanessa's, she'd returned home, determined to be more patient. To be the loving wife she wanted to be. That had entailed making an elaborate Mexican dish her mother-in-law had taught her how to prepare. "But I made your favorite."

Cruz forced a smile to his lips only because he was too tired to do it naturally. He looked at the meal. Chewing took more effort than he could give it.

"Thanks. Save it for tomorrow."

She struggled to hide her hurt. He was rejecting her. Again. "It won't taste the same."

"You made it. It'll still taste good." Cruz felt his temper threatening to spike. It took all the energy he could muster to keep it in check. "Look, I'm exhausted. If you don't mind, I'm going to turn in." He was already walking away from her toward the stairs.

"Yes, I do mind," Savannah said under her breath, but Cruz was too far away to hear.

Angry tears stung her eyes as she began to clear the table.

Two

Savannah made it upstairs less than half an hour later, after clearing the table and putting away all the untouched food. She'd gone to the trouble of cooking mainly for Cruz. The way her stomach was behaving, it didn't welcome eating no matter what time of day she tried. The best she could hope for was to keep down a few crackers at a time.

Crossing the threshold into their room, she found him facedown on the bed, his face pressed against a pillow. Cruz was sound asleep.

She sighed. Her husband looked as if he'd crashed on the bed the second he came into the room. His body was sprawled on top of the covers, his opened shirt fanned out on either side of him like denim wings. Savannah shook her head. Cruz hadn't even bothered getting undressed, except for his boots.

The air in the master bedroom was oppressively heavy. It felt sticky, still ripe with the day's humidity. Savannah walked to the windows on either side of the king-size bed and opened them as far as they would go, hoping to get a little air circulating through the room.

Nothing happened. If there was a breeze in the vicinity, it was avoiding them.

Not bothering to shed the loose-fitting sundress she had on, Savannah lay down on the other side of the bed and pretended that all was well in her life.

"Why didn't you put your nightgown on last night?"

It was the first question she heard when she walked into the kitchen the next morning.

Savannah felt groggy. Her stomach was just now inching its way down from her throat after being lodged there for the better part of the last fifteen minutes, as she'd knelt over the toilet bowl. She'd then crept down the darkened stairs, making her way through the all but pitch-black house, guided by the light coming from the kitchen.

Cruz was sitting at the table, eating. He'd fixed his own breakfast. Again.

So now she felt useless as well as harried and ignored.

"You noticed." Savannah hadn't meant to let the cryptic words escape, especially in that tone, but they had.

A piece of toast raised to his lips, Cruz looked at her as if he thought her pregnancy had somehow loosened a few screws in her head.

"Of course I noticed. You were lying right there beside me."

Savannah shrugged as she opened the refrigerator and

moved a few things around. "Since you were wearing *your* clothes, it seemed like the thing to do."

Taking out a container of milk, she poured the glassful she forced herself to drink every morning. As she raised it to her lips, she felt her stomach tighten in rebellion.

Taking her words to be a criticism, Cruz did his best to stifle the annoyance that rose up like a tidal wave inside of him. He'd never had a long fuse, but lately his temper was exceedingly short. "I was exhausted."

Savannah put the container back in the refrigerator and sat down at the table, joining him. "You're always exhausted."

His back went up, even though he continued eating. "Running a ranch takes a lot out of a man."

Savannah set the glass down after only two sips. She absolutely hated milk. "Then let someone help you run it."

He used the edge of his toast to coax the last of his scrambled eggs onto his fork. "You mean like you?" He shook his head as he took another bite. "You're already doing the bookkeeping. And you've got Luke and the house, not to mention that you're—"

Savannah cut him off. How could someone so smart be so thick? "I know exactly what I've got to do." The words rang a bit too sharply in her ears, but she couldn't seem to control the tone of her voice this morning. "And I didn't mean me. I meant one of the hands." She thought a second. "What about Paco?"

Cruz could literally feel annoyance creasing his brow. In the next minute it was gone as he reined in the frustration that seemed to appear more and more quickly these days whenever he was home.

"I told you before, Paco left." Impatience returned despite his best efforts to keep it in check. "Don't you listen to me?"

"I listen to you," she said with indignation. "I can count every word you've said to me in the last month. There haven't been many."

Was she going to start in on that again? "Look, Savannah—"

She didn't want to argue. She wanted to find a solution. Desperately, she went over the names of the other ranch hands. "What about Hank?"

Cruz stopped and stared at her. Just what was his wife up to? "Hank?"

"Why can't he share some of the burden in running the ranch?" she asked slowly. "Maybe you can make him your foreman."

He had never appointed a foreman. It was something he'd meant to do, but found himself putting off time and again. Naming a foreman meant giving someone else a share of the responsibilities that he viewed as his own. It was his ranch. His brand on everything. His good name that hung in the balance if anything went wrong.

Cruz frowned, looking down at his plate. "Hank's not ready for it."

Why not? Savannah asked herself. Just the other day her husband had mentioned how well the man was working out. Didn't Cruz remember? "He's been here almost two years—"

"I said he's not ready for it."

She pushed herself away from the table, glaring at Cruz. Damn it, he was doing this on purpose. "In your opinion, no one's ready for it. I think you're just using the ranch as an excuse not to come home to us at a decent hour."

Like a man standing on one leg on a tightrope, Cruz felt as if he was being pushed beyond his endurance. "You want decent hours, you should have married some fancy businessman who clocks in from nine to five, not me."

She stared at him. Where had that come from? There'd never been anyone but him in her life. "I didn't want a fancy businessman, I wanted you."

He caught hold of the one word that threw everything they had into jeopardy. "'Wanted?'"

"*Want.* I *still* want you," she amended, realizing what her slip must have sounded like. "But I never get to see you."

He finished his cup of coffee and put it back on its saucer. "What are you talking about? We see each other every day."

That didn't count and he knew it, Savannah thought. "For what?" she demanded. "Ten, fifteen minutes at a clip? You're always either on your way out the door or too tired to keep your eyes open."

"If that's true, how did *that* happen?" Cruz shifted his eyes toward her belly and the child who was growing there.

Picking up his plate and empty coffee cup, Savannah took both to the sink. "Once in five months doesn't count."

His manhood insulted, Cruz required a hefty dose of self-control to keep his temper and reaction in check. "It's been more than once," he corrected hotly.

She ran hot water on the plate and left it in the sink to soak for a moment. Then she shut off the tap and wiped her hands.

"You know what I mean."

"No, I don't know what you mean," he retorted, addressing his words to the back of her head. "You make it sound as if I'm having fun out there."

Tossing the towel aside, Savannah swung around. "Well, aren't you? In a way, aren't you having the time of your life out there? Horses are your first love, aren't they?"

Angry words sprang to his tongue. Cruz pressed his lips together, struggling to hold them in, knowing that once they were said, there was no way to take them back. He tried to cut her some slack because of her condition, even though she seemed bent on not cutting him any.

"I'm beginning to think the horses understand me better than you do," he said darkly.

Her eyes narrowed. They were fighting. The fight was unfolding in front of her and she felt like a bystander at a train wreck, unable to stop what was happening. Unable to curb the words that kept flying up to her lips, demanding release.

"That's probably because they get to see you more often." Taking the glass of milk, she threw the contents down the drain, then clutched the sides of the sink, trying to pull herself together. None of the words being exchanged were ones she'd meant to say this morning. She took a deep breath, trying to center herself. "Look, Cruz, I don't want to argue."

Standing up, he threw down the napkin he'd used to wipe his mouth, echoing the movement of knights of old when they threw down a glove as a silent challenge.

"For a woman who doesn't want to argue, you do a damn poor job of reaching your goal."

And then, because he truly did love her, Cruz made his own attempt to smooth things out. Maybe he hadn't been supportive enough, but hell, he was busier than God these days. Every time he turned around, there were more bills to face, more problems to smooth out. And that didn't even include the training. Cutting horses required a great deal of time and attention.

"Look," he began again, "you're pregnant. Your hormones or whatever are all over the map. Why don't you leave Luke with one of my sisters today and take a bubble bath or something?"

As if soapy water could somehow magically change everything between them, she thought.

Well, she amended, maybe it could at that. Or at least it could help her take a stab at starting over.

Turning from the sink, she crossed to him, then smiled. "I'd like to take a bubble bath. With you."

He felt the effects of her smile. It was like watching sunshine rise over a darkened land. "That's too girlie."

Another wave of nausea threatened to overtake her. Savannah concentrated on pushing it back. This was far more important. She wound her arms around her husband's neck, playing with the dark locks of hair at his collar.

"Not if I'm in the tub with you…"

He could feel the heat from her body. The heat from his own. "Yeah, well…"

Sensing her advantage, Savannah pressed herself against him, her eyes taking him prisoner. "Like we used to, Cruz."

"We never took a bubble bath together," he protested, but not too vehemently.

"No," she agreed, grinning. "But we took showers together. Don't you remember soaping up each other's bodies?" Her voice was soft, low. It stirred him. "Don't you remember what it was like, Cruz, drying each other off?"

His body was rebelling, betraying him. Now wasn't the time or the place! "Savannah, you know you're making me crazy."

"Am I, Cruz? Am I?" Hope lit a tiny candle in the dark center of her soul. She pressed her body against his, feeling the imprint of it along her own. Feeling him harden. She had him, she thought in heady triumph. She just needed to press her advantage. "Why don't you take the morning off? We can drop Luke off at one of your sisters, just like you said." She raised herself on her toes, her face turned up to his. "Spend a little time together."

Her mouth was seductively close. Temptation leaped out at him, taking hold.

He wasn't made out of stone and he loved his wife. From the moment she'd returned to the Double Crown Ranch, there hadn't been another woman around who could even remotely tempt him. He didn't want anyone else. It was as if he'd buried that part of him that had searched for answers in other women's beds. Savannah was the only answer he'd ever wanted or needed.

But right now he was needed elsewhere, not here, giving in to his own desires.

Cruz struggled to hold himself back. He knew that if he gave in to the ever-increasing wave of desire within him, if he even kissed Savannah, he'd be sunk.

He couldn't afford to let that happen. There was so much to do today.

Very gently, he took hold of the arms around his neck and untangled himself from her. He saw the confusion, the disappointment in her eyes and felt something twist within his gut.

But she'd been his wife for over five years now. She understood about this life they led. What was required. "Honey, I just can't today. I've got five new horses coming in."

Frustrated beyond words, she wanted to scream, to rant. For the first time in her life, she wanted to throw a full-scale tantrum. "And you have to greet them personally?"

He tried to put his hand on her shoulder, but she shrugged him off. They were back in their corners again. "Savannah, you know better than that."

Stepping away from him, she sighed. "Yes, I know better than that."

He couldn't stand to see the sadness in her eyes. Allowing himself one final moment before hurrying out the door, Cruz paused to take her chin in his hand. Tilting her head back just a little, he lightly brushed his lips over hers.

"Soon," he promised. "Just be patient a bit longer."

"What choice do I have?" Savannah murmured, feeling dejected. She saw another endless, frustrating, lonely day stretch out in front of her. A day without Cruz. She dearly loved her son, but she needed a break from him. A break from him and time with her husband. But that wasn't going to happen.

Her eyes met Cruz's, willing him to stay. "I love you."

"And I love you," he told her. "This is all for you, you know that. For you and Luke." Grabbing his hat, he started to leave the kitchen.

"No," she said sadly to his back. "It's all for you. Because I could live in a mud hut, as long as you were right there beside me."

Wearily, Cruz spun on his heel to look at her. She was spouting romantic nonsense and he was in no mood for it. "No," he said evenly, "you couldn't. Because you can't wear mud, you can't eat mud, you can't hand a bucket of mud to the doctor. It takes money, Savannah. Everything takes money and I'm earning it the only way I know how."

And he was getting damn tired of having to justify himself to her on top of everything else he had to do. "Go call one of my sisters. Take that bubble bath," he instructed. "You'll feel better."

She said nothing as the sound of his boots receding on the wooden floor echoed through the silent house. The next moment, she heard the front door closing.

"No, I won't," she countered. "The only thing that will make me feel better is knowing that you're still in love with me."

And she had grave doubts about that. Doubts that her giving in to her heart and marrying Cruz had been the right thing to do, after all.

Maybe she had made a mistake.

She'd held out in the beginning because she hadn't wanted what her parents had had. Theirs was a marriage forged by guilt, held together by desperation, and eventually disintegrated by mutual loathing. All because they'd set out to "do the right thing" in the beginning. Her mother had been pregnant with her when she and her father had gotten married, and not a day went by in her childhood that they allowed her to forget it. To forget that she was the reason for their misery.

She had grown up feeling responsible for generating the unhappiness of not just one person, but two. She'd also grown up vowing that when it was her turn, she was not going to marry for any other reason than love.

Everlasting love.

And when she'd looked into Cruz's ruggedly handsome face, that was exactly what she'd felt. She'd known that she was always going to love him all the days of her life, no matter what.

But as far as being assured that he would feel the same…well, that had taken some convincing on his part. But he'd worn her down, making her believe that he truly wanted her, not because it was the honorable thing to do, but because he loved her.

Maybe he was a better actor than she'd given him credit for.

Or maybe she'd just talked herself into it. After all, if Cruz did love her, would he be using the ranch as an excuse to be away from her except for a few hours a day? Would he be so caught up in his horses that he didn't have any time to spare for her or the child he'd given his name to?

Cruz had been extremely fussy when it came to hiring men to work on his ranch. Right now they had three very capable hands, two who lived on the property in a mobile trailer Cruz's parents had given them. Men he'd told her he relied on.

So why wasn't he delegating any responsibility to them? Why did he have to be personally involved in every single tiny aspect of running the ranch? He was so completely hands-on. From the feeding and handling of the horses right down to the maintenance of the fences that kept his herd of twenty-five within the five-hundred-acre ranch, he was there for everything.

First one up, last one down.

It was as if he had something to prove. Over and over again, every day. As if he was the last man hired instead of the one who handed out the paychecks.

Despite the summer heat, which was still stifling in the early-morning hours, Savannah poured hot water over the tea bag she'd plunked into her cup. Maybe tea would help soothe her stomach, although she didn't hold out much hope.

She took the cup back to the table, hoping to pull herself together before Luke bounced out of bed.

Clutching the cup with both hands, she brought it to her lips and blew before taking the smallest sip and letting the liquid wind down into her stomach.

Granted, she'd known when she married Cruz that he would never be a gentleman rancher. That he wouldn't be just marginally involved in the day-to-day activities but would plunge into them, full steam ahead. That was what she loved about him—that he could get involved with something wholeheartedly.

She just never thought that it would ultimately be to the exclusion of her and their child.

Cruz had been a horse whisperer when she'd first met him, a man who had an almost uncanny affinity for the animals he trained. He could take a horse with a broken spirit, a horse that seemed infused with the very devil himself, and somehow find a way to reach the animal. To form a bond and communicate with it until that animal had completely transformed into a horse that could be trained, managed. A horse that any owner would be proud to have.

First Cruz would breach the chasm, then became one with the horse, and the horse would become one with him. It was a thing of beauty to watch.

But now it seemed that he had thrown her over for the horses.

The horses and everything that went with them. The care, the cleaning, the feeding and the mucking out of the stalls, every aspect of the animals' lives came before sharing time with his family.

And she hadn't a clue how to change that.

Savannah felt tears stinging her eyes. How had she lost him?

Why didn't he love her as he used to?

She thought of the tiny moment they'd shared just before he'd left. The old Cruz was still in there somewhere. She just needed to find a way to bring him out again.

To have him want her again.

Savannah glanced at her reflection in the darkened window just above the sink as the first rays of dawn began to materialize along the horizon. She turned sideways, critically studying herself. Her body wasn't misshapen yet.

Maybe she could seduce him.

A hopeful smile curved her lips. The idea had merit.

Three

The second Savannah finished making the last of the new entries into the computer program she used to track La Esperanza's expenses, she saved the data and turned off her computer.

Closing the laptop, she turned toward her son, who was still very enamored with the action figures Vanessa had given him yesterday. Both monster and monster eradicator were making awful noises, courtesy of Luke. Any other time it might have been enough to get a bad headache rolling in Savannah's skull.

But not today. She had a plan to get rolling instead. And a marriage to get back on track.

Glancing at Luke, she saw that he was perched on top of the sofa, a figure in each hand. Obviously the fantasy he was acting out had taken the two characters and their orchestrator up to the top of some mountain.

"You know the rules, Luke," she called out to him. "No flying off the sofa."

Clutching his figures to him, he pushed out his bottom lip. "Aw, Mama."

She gave him her best no-nonsense look. "No 'aw, Mama.' Down, mister."

Luke scooted his bottom down along the upholstery, then scrambled off the cushion. Before she could blink, he was on the floor, using the massive coffee table as a new battlefield.

Satisfied that Luke was safe for a nanosecond, she picked up the receiver and dialed Rosita's home phone. Her mother-in-law was always her first choice when it came to Luke. The woman and her husband doted on the boy. If, by some wild chance, Rosita and Ruben were busy tonight, she knew she could always fall back on any one of her four sisters-in-law, or Vanessa, for that matter. Luke felt equally comfortable with all of them.

Tonight, Savannah decided, her firstborn was going to be sleeping in a bed other than his own. And she was going to reclaim what was rightfully hers.

Theirs, she amended, as she listened to the phone on the other end ringing. Because Cruz had been happy once, too. Happy making love with her. Happy with just loving her, the way she did him.

All married couples went through doldrums, Savannah told herself as she silently counted off the number of times the phone rang. Discord was only natural. It was up to her to see that they carved out a little island of time for themselves, recharged their batteries, so to speak.

It wasn't that she had less to do than Cruz. In her own way, she firmly believed that she had just as much if not more to do than the man she'd promised to give her love to for all eternity. He had the ranch to run, she had everything else to run. The house, the books, their son and any emergency that might come up.

But then, women were far more resilient than their male counterparts and capable of multitasking on top of that. Ordinarily she was that way herself, when she wasn't pregnant. Lately, though, she kept flagging, as if she couldn't hang on to her energy for more than a few minutes at a time.

She didn't remember being this exhausted when she was carrying Luke.

The phone on the other end was finally picked up. She straightened, eager to set her plan in motion.

"Hello, Mama?" The woman had insisted that she call her Mama after the wedding, and in truth, Savannah felt closer to Rosita than she ever had to her own mother. The name rolled easily from her tongue.

"Savannah?" There was immediate concern in the other woman's voice. "What's wrong?"

Savannah did her best to sound as cheerful as possible. Anything less and Rosita would be over in a flash, thinking the worst. It was Rosita's belief that she had far too much happiness in her life, and she was always anticipating a reversal.

"Nothing's wrong, Mama. I was just wondering if you'd mind taking your grandson for the night?"

"You know I'd love to have Luke over here anytime, but why tonight? Are you two going somewhere?"

To paradise, I hope. Savannah gauged her words carefully, not sure just how much Cruz would appreciate her telling her mother-in-law. He was very proud and this might offend his sense of independence. "Cruz has been working very hard lately—"

She could almost see Rosita nodding her dark head in agreement. "Takes a lot to run a ranch."

"Yes, I know, he said the same thing." Savannah suppressed the sigh that tried to rise to her lips. "But he's forgotten how to unwind."

"Unwind?"

The woman was probably unfamiliar with the term. "To relax. To enjoy himself." Savannah paused. Then, because she liked the woman and because she had a feeling that Rosita would guess anyway, she added, "To be a husband again."

Rosita caught on immediately, as Savannah knew she would. "Ah, I see. Of course. I can have Ruben come by and pick the boy up now if you'd like. It would give me extra time with my beautiful grandson—and you extra time to do whatever it is you need to do to help Cruz…unwind."

Savannah didn't want to seem as if she was eager to ship her son off, but in reality, Rosita had a good point. She'd get twice as much done without having Luke in tow. "Well…"

"Consider it done," Rosita said, taking the decision out of her daughter-in-law's hands. "Ruben will be there in less than half an hour. Have Luke and his favorite toys ready. And, Savannah?"

"Yes?"

"Good luck."

"Thank you." She didn't bother commenting that if she had to rely on luck to make Cruz come around, then her marriage really was in serious trouble.

* * *

Cruz was well pleased.

The four quarter horses he'd arranged to buy looked even better walking off the back of the transport than they had when he had first seen them running free on Eric Tyler's ranch. All four were fine specimens of their breed. And intelligent.

He could tell that the horses he'd picked were intelligent just by moving among them, the way he was now. He was getting a bead on them and they were getting one on him. He liked that.

Nothing worse than a dumb animal, he thought, at least for what he had in mind. He trained quarter horses to become cutting horses, animals specifically intended to herd cattle. A good horse could even prevent a stampede from getting under way, separating one frightened steer from the others before the mindless pounding of hooves and the surge of escape began.

Not that he couldn't handle an animal blessed with less than the intelligence he saw on display today. Very slowly, he wound a lariat around his arm as he eyed the newest additions to his herd.

He had a way of communicating with horses that at times surprised even him. Had he been one of the Plains Indians, he might have said he was bonding with his brothers. But no such thought crossed Cruz's mind when he walked into the small, tight corral to transform yet another horse from a skittish, rebellious animal to one that was willing to work for its master. To bring the fruit of its abilities to the man or woman who fed and cared for him or her.

However, something happened when Cruz was alone

with a horse, something he could not explain. Something that almost allowed him to form a spiritual bond with the creature, to feel what the horse was feeling, to understand what caused its distrust or its pain.

When he had worked for the Double Crown, he had been given the toughest horses to break. Horses that had long since been given up on were brought to him in hopes that he could turn them around.

He'd never had a single failure. Sometime it took weeks, even months, but the object was not to rush, rather to succeed.

That was when he'd had the luxury of working for someone else, however. Now that he was his own master, now that what he accomplished put food on his table and clothes on the backs of his family, it was a slightly different matter. There was an urgency inside of him, an urgency to succeed, to build up the ranch, as well as his reputation. To have the kind of things he had always dreamed about having, not because he wanted them—he couldn't care less about fancy cars or pricey clothing—but because those outer trappings meant that he, Cruz Perez, was a success.

A man to respect.

A man who could not only compete in a world populated by the likes of the Fortunes, but could also carve out a sizable place for himself.

That took dedication and work, tireless work. Not an easy matter when he was far from tireless. Especially when he walked into the house and heard recriminations thrown his way. Or when he saw the disappointment in Savannah's eyes.

She never seemed happy anymore when he did have a moment to spend with her. That meant he was failing her somehow. More than anything else, he didn't like failing.

A fifth horse was being led off the transport. The hand was having a difficult time bringing him over to the corral. This was the horse that Tyler had thrown in for a song.

"You'll be doing me a favor taking it off my hands," Eric Tyler had told him. Tugging off his hat, the older man had scratched his thinning hair and shaken his head. "I purely don't know what to do with him."

Even though he'd seen the other four as a sound investment of his time and money, Cruz had been drawn to the last animal immediately.

There was something about the black horse, an air that separated him from the others. There was the same amount of intelligence in its eyes as the other four—more, really—but also something else. A wariness coupled with fire.

He seemed almost human.

This one, Cruz had thought, watching as several of Tyler's hands scattered after trying to herd the horse into a smaller corral, was a prize. A warrior.

Turning him into a working cutting horse wouldn't be easy.

But Cruz loved a challenge.

"What's his name?" he had asked, approaching the corral.

"Diablo," Tyler had told him.

Diablo. The devil. It fit.

Inside the corral now, Diablo shook his proud head, his deep brown eyes locking with Cruz's across the length of the field. Cruz found himself smiling.

"You think you'll come out on top, don't you?" he murmured almost to himself. "You're in for a surprise, my friend."

But taming and training Diablo was going to take time, and right now he needed to get busy with the four he'd purchased. He had a contract with the Flying W to turn over four fully trained cutting horses by the end of the month. That meant focusing his day a little differently, but it could be done.

The July sun beat down mercilessly.

Cruz could feel the line of sweat forming around the rim of his worn Stetson. Taking it off, he wiped his brow, then set the hat back on his head as his eyes swept over the field. One of his hands was still in the stables, mucking the stalls out before spreading a fresh layer of straw. The other two were caring for the horses that had been led into the corral. Horses needed to be washed down, especially in this heat.

Two of his mares were expecting. One had given birth to a dead colt last year. He hoped that her luck would be better this time around. There wasn't anything to do but wait and see.

A thousand details to keep tabs on.

He thought about what Savannah had said about Hank. That he should consider making the wrangler a foreman. That he should give serious thought to entrusting others with more responsibility rather than shouldering it all himself. It would make life easier, he thought. But it was just that he did everything better than anyone.

It wasn't vanity that prompted his feelings, it was training and ability. He'd been a cowboy all of his life, and he knew exactly what it took to run a ranch. He'd waited all his life for the chance.

And here it was.

Still, he knew damn well that he couldn't be everywhere at once. When it came to the daily chores, he figured he'd be safe enough assigning those to the others without having to stand over them to make sure everything was taken care of. Feeding, bathing, exercising the horses and cleaning out their stalls took time. Cruz made up his mind to allow the others to take care of those details.

But training the horses, putting them through their paces until he was satisfied that they were the best they could be, was another matter entirely. Training horses was careful, almost artistic work. That was his domain.

Still, he had to start letting go somewhere, he thought. Going into Red Rock was on his agenda today, but he couldn't do that and get the horses comfortable around him at the same time. He looked toward where a tall, rail-thin cowboy with bright red hair stood talking to another hand. Catching the redhead's eye, he waved the man over.

"Hank, we need some more horse liniment and I'm going to have to buy saddles for these four. Why don't you take one of the boys and go into Red Rock and pick them up for me?" He took the ranch credit card out of his wallet and handed it to Hank. "And while you're at it, we're running low on feed."

"Yes, I know." Taking off his hat, Hank ran a hand through his hair. He looked at his boss a little uncertainly, as if he wasn't sure he'd heard him correctly. It was a known fact that Cruz, although a fair man, was a control freak. "You want me to pick out the saddles?"

Cruz took Hank's hesitant look to mean that he wasn't up to the task. But since he'd asked him to handle it, he couldn't very well back off. "Why? Don't you feel you can?"

"Well, hell, yeah, they're only saddles." He looked at Cruz curiously. "But you always wanted to do it before."

Cruz blew out a breath. This letting go wasn't going to

be easy, no matter what Savannah thought. She was clearly the smarter one, he'd give her that, but he was the one who knew what it took to operate a ranch. Still, he supposed he owed it to her to give this some kind of trial run.

"I'm delegating." The word felt like hardened peanut brittle in his mouth. "Something my wife keeps telling me I should do."

Hank nodded his head, no doubt pleased with the idea. A grin curved his mouth. "Well, seeing as how you're 'delegating' stuff, I could help you with the training." He nodded toward the corral, where all five horses stood, four in relatively close proximity and Diablo over to the side.

It was no secret that Hank had set his cap on becoming a trainer, that he'd spent hours of his free time watching Cruz as he put horses through their paces.

But Cruz knew watching and feeling an instinct were two different things. You couldn't learn instinct. Even the thought of sharing the responsibility of training the horses didn't sit well with him.

"I'll keep it in mind," he replied, in the same tone of voice that parents used to make children believe they had a ghost of a chance of something coming true, when in reality the exact opposite was more likely.

Hank ran his hand along his neck, nodding. The look in his eyes when they met Cruz's said he knew that what he'd just suggested wasn't about to happen anytime soon.

Hank blew out a breath as he set his hat far back on his head. "Yeah, well, it was just a thought." Putting the credit card into his shirt pocket, he stuck his hands into his back pockets. "Want me to take the Mustang?"

"No, take the truck," Cruz told him. He dug the keys out

of his jeans and tossed them to the other man. "You're going to need the space," he added.

"Yeah, right."

Hank closed his hand around the keys. Walking off toward the parking area, he called one of the other hands over to join him in his trip to Red Rock.

Watching him go, Cruz frowned.

The man hadn't even asked to take the proper vehicle. How was Cruz going to make him a foreman if he didn't have enough sense to take a truck instead of a small, vintage Mustang when he went to get four saddles and fresh feed for the horses?

And this was the man Savannah wanted him to put in charge directly under him? No way. Cruz was going to have to stay on top of everything—unless he wanted La Esperanza to quickly become the property of the bank that held its mortgage.

He knew he had to get started, but he took a second to walk over to Diablo. The stallion was at the far end of the corral, separating himself from the other quarter horses as if he knew he was special.

No failure of ego here, Cruz thought, amused.

He climbed up to the top rung of the fence, holding on to it as he leaned over the railing. Eyeing him, the horse took a few steps back, but not enough to display fear. The horse, Cruz sensed, had a will every bit as strong as his own.

That made them both fighters.

"This is your new home, Diablo. You'd better get used to it."

As if to show that he understood and that he was displeased, the stallion pawed the ground, tossing his mane in a gesture that could only be called defiant.

In a way, Cruz knew how he felt. As a young man, he'd refused to allow himself to be sublimated into the Fortunes' world, even though for the most part he both liked and respected the members of the family.

Sublimation was for his parents, but not for him.

"You'd better know now," he told Diablo, "that kind of behavior doesn't put me off. You might have been top dog at the last ranch, but you've met your match here. We're going to get together, you and me, and be friends. That's a promise."

He made no attempt to reach out to touch the horse, or even to enter the corral. The horse required his space. For now Cruz would respect that. But the animal did need to get accustomed to his presence in his world.

Training would begin early tomorrow morning, before he even started working with the others. Half an hour, twice a day. He didn't have the time, but he'd find it. Even if it meant doing some more delegating.

An excitement pulsed through Cruz. He hadn't felt this alive in a long time.

While watching her reflection in the wardrobe mirror, Savannah realized that her hands were shaking ever so slightly as she smoothed the sides of her dress.

She stared down at her hands. They were also tingling. And damp.

She shook her head and silently laughed at herself. You'd think she was going out on her first date. There had to be a hundred butterflies all vying for airspace inside her stomach.

For once, she didn't feel like collapsing or throwing up. The newest Perez-in-the-making had decided, for now, to cooperate with its mother.

Thank God for small favors, she thought.

The moment her father-in-law had come for Luke, she'd dashed off to Red Rock to buy things for the dinner she wanted to make for Cruz.

But before going to the supermarket, she'd stopped by the mall. Not to buy a new dress, but a new nightgown. Something just sheer enough to get his blood pumping in double time.

She'd picked out a full-length one that had a network of lace across her breasts and two layers of sheer, light blue nylon swirling around her hips down to the floor.

She couldn't wait to see the expression on Cruz's face when she wore it.

Returning home, she'd cleaned the house and started dinner going before finally going upstairs to change out of her jeans and into her dress for the evening.

Right now she had both dinner and herself warming, waiting for Cruz to make his appearance. She glanced at the clock. It was a little after seven.

She'd already called him on the cell phone she'd insisted he carry with him when he was on the range. It had taken eight rings before he'd finally answered. The second he came on, she'd launched her assault.

"Cruz, I need you to come home."

The preoccupied note immediately left his voice, replaced by concern. "Why? What's wrong? Did something happen to Luke?"

"No, nothing happened to Luke—"

"You? Did something happen to you? Is it the baby?"

"No, honey," she interjected before his imagination took him to terrible places. "It's not the baby, or me. Luke and I are fine."

"Then why are you calling?"

She never used the telephone to get in touch with him. They had agreed that it was strictly for emergencies. As far as she was concerned, saving a marriage that was about to break apart came under that heading.

"Because I do have kind of an emergency here and I need you to come home."

Suspicion and concern vied in his voice. "What kind of an emergency?"

"It's too hard to explain, Cruz. You'll understand when you get here. Please just hurry."

She'd heard him sigh. "Okay, I'm on my way."

That had been over half an hour ago.

Obviously the man was a lot farther away that she'd thought. Savannah reached for the cell phone again, then stopped. She heard the sound of the Mustang pulling up to the front of the house.

He was here.

Butterflies launched another attack as she took a deep breath and waited.

Within a moment, Cruz was opening the front door. "Okay, so what's the big emergency?"

The question faded into the air as Savannah moved out of the shadows to greet him. She was wearing the same drop-dead gorgeous dress she'd had on the night he'd met her at the party at the Double Crown.

The night he'd lost his heart to her.

Four

Feeling a little like a man who had just stepped through some kind of time warp, Cruz closed the door slowly behind him. There was music wafting from somewhere on the first floor. Something soft and romantic, setting the mood.

Nodding a greeting, he continued staring at the deep green clingy dress. Memories came crowding back, bringing with them feelings he hadn't entertained in a long time.

Fear that she was ill melted into anger at being taken away from his work under false pretenses, then finally ebbed into confusion. "What's this all about?"

She couldn't gauge his reaction by his tone. It gave nothing away.

Savannah forced herself to erase five years of marriage from her conscious behavior. Tonight she was not the frustrated wife and harried mother she'd been for so long she couldn't easily remember what it was like otherwise. Tonight she was attending a party at her friend Vanessa's house and had just seen the most beautiful man she'd ever laid eyes on.

A man who radiated sheer animal magnetism with every move he made, every smoldering look he sent her way. From the first moment she'd seen him, Cruz Perez had made her blood rush through her veins just by being near. She desperately needed to recapture that sensation.

Needed to recapture, too, that essence within herself that had made him want her so much he was willing to forsake all the others who had come before her. And those who wanted to come after her.

With slow, measured steps, taken in strappy high heels that were, if she wore them at all, usually shed the second she walked in the front door, Savannah moved toward him. She looked every bit the huntress who had staked out her next prey and was confident of its capture.

Never mind that she was nervous, that she was afraid he'd laugh at her efforts, that she feared that what they'd had was now behind them. She masked those worries and did her best to look like a determined woman.

A determined, sexy woman.

"It's about getting to know each other," she told him in a sultry voice.

Well, this was new. Cruz looked at her a little uncertainly. "You feeling all right, Savannah?"

"I'm fine."

She trailed the back of her hand along his face, then slid her fingertips down his throat, lingering where it dipped in. Savannah became aware of his pulse. It felt as if it had accelerated.

Good!

Before she could press it against his chest, Cruz caught her hand and held it for a moment. Savannah was stirring things up and he wanted to be able to think clearly.

"Then what's this talk about getting to know each other?" he asked her. "We already know each other. I know everything about you and you damn well know everything about me."

He had no secrets from her. She was the other half of his soul, and filled his thoughts. Didn't she know that?

"Everything?" Savannah teased, her breath dancing along his cheek.

She moved her head nearer, bringing her lips achingly close to his. At the last possible second she drew back, just when she judged Cruz was going to kiss her. A little effort, a little pursuit helped to spice things up. She didn't want this to be too easy, even though part of her wanted to throw herself into his arms and make love right here and now until there wasn't a breath left within her body.

The look in her eyes challenged him as she took him up on his claim. "If you know me inside and out, what color underwear am I wearing?"

What had come over her? He spread his hands wide, trying to harness his confusion. "I don't know." And then, because she looked as if she was waiting for some kind of an answer, he gave one. "White?"

She moved her head from side to side slowly, her eyes never leaving his. "No."

He made another stab, picking her favorite color. "Blue?"

That was the color of the nightgown she was going to wear for him tonight. If clouds could be called blue. "No."

Exasperated, he held back his temper. "Okay, then, what color?"

Instead of answering, she took his hand and lightly placed it against her hip. With her eyes on his, her hand covering his, she slowly rotated his palm toward her buttocks.

Savannah watched with pleasure as a light came into her husband's eyes. He lifted his brow as a surprised, sensual smile came to his lips.

"You're not wearing any."

"The man gets a prize." She moved her body against his, silently indicating that she was the prize he had won.

Tired though he was, Cruz could feel himself responding to her. After all, until life and its myriad details had caught up to them and dragged them both down, burying them beneath a ton of responsibilities that only insisted on multiplying, they'd had an incredible sex life.

For all her innocence, Savannah had turned out to be the best natural lover he'd ever had. Considering the fact that he was far from a novice, this was saying a great deal.

Yearning seized him the way it hadn't for a long time. But even as he lowered his mouth to hers, Cruz suddenly stopped himself and looked around uneasily.

"What's wrong?" Didn't he want her anymore? The question feverishly throbbed in her head, ushering fear in its wake.

"Honey, what if Luke walks in on us?"

She offered up a silent prayer of thanks. He *did* want her, he was just being a good father. Her mouth softened into a smile. "Then I'd ask him what a five-year-old was doing walking all the way over from the other side of Red Rock."

Cruz's brows knitted together in a confused line. "I don't—"

Poor darling, he really was tired, not to immediately make the connection.

But not so tired that she hadn't gotten to him, Savannah congratulated herself. She could feel his body hardening. Wanting her. At least she still appealed to him, she thought with not a little relief. She'd begun to have her doubts.

"Our son is staying at your parents' house tonight, bless them. Your dad came by earlier today to pick him up."

Cruz stiffened slightly. "You told them you were doing this?"

She knew what a private man her husband had turned out to be, even about something as natural as this. She framed her words carefully. "I told them we needed some time alone together. Maybe they think we're painting the baby's room."

Cruz laughed and shook his head, relaxing. "My parents are not dumb people."

No, they were smart beyond books and very in tune to what was happening around them. She'd seen more than one display of affection between her in-laws. Not like with her own parents. All the years she'd spent growing up, she had never witnessed so much as a chaste kiss between the two. The only thing that had ever been remotely hot had been the words they had thrown at each other.

"Maybe that's why your parents have such a long, healthy marriage."

Cruz took her into his arms, toying with the tendrils of hair along her neck. How long had it been since he'd seen her like this? Soft, relaxed, stirring. "You saying our marriage isn't healthy?"

It wasn't terminal, Savannah thought, but it certainly was ill. Using humor, she allowed snippets of honesty to come through.

"I'm saying it's in danger of having rigor mortis set in." Savannah wiggled against him, deliberately tempting him. "Use it or lose it. The way I see it—" she let her eyes dip down his torso "—all the parts are still under original warranty."

"Okay, let's see what we can do about wearing out a few of those parts." Cupping her face, Cruz lowered his mouth to hers. He was utterly surprised when, instead of kissing him, Savannah moved back and took a few steps away from him. Confused, he stared at her. "Now what?"

Savannah nodded toward the dining room behind her. "We eat first."

"Eat?" He said the word as if he didn't fully fathom what it meant.

Turning on her heel, she began to lead the way. "I made all your favorites—"

Cruz caught her hand, turning her around again until she faced him. "Good, then let me start by sampling my *very* favorite." He kissed her shoulder, causing the butterflies that had been in her stomach to spread their wings and take to the air.

Her very skin was sizzling.

It was working.

He was beginning to sound the way he had when she'd first met him. When she'd first married him. He'd been sexier than hell back then. All she wanted was to have him back, and now here he was.

She moved out of his reach again. "I want to draw this out, make it last."

He winked at her, that grin she loved so much curving his mouth. "I'll do my very best."

A laugh bubbled up in her throat. "I meant by eating dinner first." As if to mark his place for him, Savannah leaned into Cruz and lightly brushed her lips against his. When he started to kiss her, she pulled back. "Dessert will be served upstairs."

Cruz caught her in his arms and kissed her, his mouth hard against hers. The kiss made her melt. Made her body temperature rise several degrees in wild anticipation of what was to come.

They hadn't made love in so long, she'd lost count of the days. Of the weeks.

She could feel her body rejoicing.

Savannah wound her arms around his neck, cleaving to the warmth of him, losing herself in the mind-spinning effect that his mouth had always had on her. To hell with her carefully laid plans; she was seizing the moment.

And then she felt his hands on her shoulders, moving her back.

Stunned, dazed, she all but stumbled backward. It took her a second to focus on his face.

Cruz smiled, pleased at what he saw. Two could play the game she'd come up with, and maybe she had something there at that. Maybe making her the slightest bit unattainable did heighten the stakes, did increase the anticipation rather than simply gratifying himself instantly.

He was willing to go along with that, even though, when he'd walked into the house, he'd been more tired than an eagle after a three-day, nonstop flight.

He loved seeing the effect of his kiss on her, loved seeing how her lips were pink and slightly swollen. "Consider that a retainer."

It took Savannah a moment to process his words. And then she laughed. "I want payment in full, the second we cross that threshold."

He gave her a quick, two-finger salute. "Consider it done."

As he walked with her into the dining room, Cruz placed his hand on her hip, silently reaffirming not just the emotional but the physical bond that existed between them.

About to sit down, he stopped himself at the last moment and went to help Savannah with her chair. Her surprised look melted into a pleased one, making the extra effort worth it.

When had all the niceties eroded between them? Had they been erased by the comfort of familiarity, or had he and his wife just become too tired to care?

This was better, he thought.

"Everything smells good," he stated as he sat down. "Especially you."

There was hope, she told herself, pleased that she'd thought to do this. Pleased with his response. She'd begun to think that maybe they had gotten beyond salvaging. That they'd become an old married couple years before their time, taking each other for granted and just existing side by side instead of actually living each moment fully the way they had when they'd first gotten married.

"Thank you," she murmured. Pleasure brought color to her cheeks. She could feel it spreading.

Cruz flashed her an apologetic smile as he helped himself to the burritos rancheros Savannah had carefully arranged in the serving dish. They were smothered in sour cream and guacamole sauce. He took a good portion of each.

"I'm afraid I smell a little ripe."

She grinned. That had never bothered her about him. "I don't mind a little perspiration," she told him. "On you, it's a very manly smell."

He put the spatula back in the dish. "You're easy to please."

Her eyes met his. God, but she loved this man. "In some ways," she agreed, then felt compelled to add, "in others, not so easy."

There was chilled wine waiting on his pleasure. He took only a little, feeling bad that she couldn't have any. The wine felt good as it slid down his throat, enhancing the mood.

"Is that a riddle?" he asked, setting his glass down.

"You can work it out later." Her voice was low, husky, full of promise.

To his surprise, Cruz felt himself getting excited again.

He found himself hurrying through the meal, barely aware of what he was eating, only that it was tasty. His plate was cleaned within fifteen minutes of sitting down at the table, the contents washed down by a little more wine.

Cruz noticed that Savannah's plate was clean, as well. But in her case it was because she'd taken next to nothing to begin with.

He nodded toward her plate as he pushed his own back. "Not hungry?"

She gave a little shrug, the light dancing off her bare shoulders. "I ate while I was making it."

It was a lie, but one that she was allowed, she thought. If she made him aware of just how little she consumed during the course of a day, he'd worry. The truth was, she was afraid that if she ate more than the small portion of plain rice she'd prepared for herself, all her plans for the evening ahead would be ruined.

There was little doubt in Savannah's mind that she would wind up spending the night in the bathroom, being ill.

As it was, ever since she'd become pregnant with her second child, waves of nausea kept assaulting her at the most inopportune times. They were at their most predictable shortly after a meal.

Shortly after this meal, she intended to be naked and entertaining her husband, as well as being entertained by him. A sudden run to the commode did not come under that heading.

Finished with his meal, Cruz began to rise with his plate.

His mother, Savannah mused, had trained this man well. But tonight that didn't make any points.

"Leave it," she told him, guiding the plate back to the table. "They'll keep."

Rising to her feet, she took his hand and began to walk toward the stairs.

He surprised her by abruptly stopping in the foyer before the staircase, just shy of the living room. When she turned around to look at him quizzically, Cruz took her into his arms.

Ever so slowly, he began to sway with her, in time to the music.

"We danced that first night, remember?" He enveloped her hand with his own, pressing it against his chest as he danced.

Against his heart, she thought, feeling the rhythm of its beat.

"On the terrace," he continued. "Music from the party was drifting out of all the opened windows, and we danced the last time you wore this dress."

That he remembered such a small detail thrilled her beyond measure.

"Yes," she said softly, leaning her cheek against his chest, "I remember."

Anticipation paired off with adrenaline, creating all sorts of delicious havoc within her body as she moved to the strains of the slow love song. She was happy enough to cry.

Damn her hormones, she thought. The smile didn't leave her lips.

"This was a good idea." Cruz's breath wafted through her hair.

Raising her head, she looked up at him. She loved him so much, she thought, that it hurt. "Glad you liked it."

The song ended and he kissed her. Lightly, briefly, whetting both their appetites. Releasing her, he made no effort to step back.

She sighed and their breath mingled. Something in his belly tightened. Cruz glanced toward the stairs.

"As I remember, you were leading me somewhere before I stopped to claim a dance."

Her eyes were fairly dancing themselves as she smiled, taking his hand again. "Yes, I was."

This time they made it up the stairs.

As they crossed the threshold into their bedroom, Cruz again pulled her into his arms. "I believe I have a promise to make good on."

"Wait," she cried, placing her hands against his chest. "Give me some time."

With an impatient sigh, Cruz released her. "I *have* been waiting," he pointed out. "And the way I see it, time is now being wasted."

She thought of the nightgown she'd hung up so carefully on the back of the bathroom door. The one that was going to make his jaw drop. "I want to put something on."

A small, perturbed frown appeared on his lips. Maybe he just wasn't following her. "I thought the object was to take something off."

She laughed, giving him a quick kiss. "Trust me, this is worth waiting for."

Cruz sighed again, but the look of impatience was gone. "Just don't make the wait too long, Savannah," he warned. He let his eyes slide down the length of her body. There was no way anyone would have suspected she was pregnant. She looked just the way she had that first night. His own body tightened again in response as thoughts filled his head. "I'm not sure how much longer I'm going to be able to hold out."

She laughed just before she slipped into the bathroom. "Just don't start without me."

The moment the door was closed, Savannah quickly stripped off her dress. She hung it carefully on a hanger and then slipped on the sexy blue nightgown she'd bought just for this moment.

Stepping all the way back against the far wall, she critically surveyed her reflection in the medicine cabinet mirror one last time.

All the right curves were still there, she thought with satisfaction.

She'd worked hard at getting herself back into shape after Luke was born. It had been worth all those endless hours of exercise she'd managed to string together.

She was going to knock Cruz on his ear.

Running a comb through her hair, she placed it back into the medicine cabinet and then opened the door.

"Here I come, Cruz," she announced. "Ready or not."

There was no answer.

Puzzled, Savannah stepped into their bedroom. Cruz was lying down on the bed with his back to her. The television had been turned on, though the sound was low. He'd obviously decided that she was going to be in there for a while.

A lot he knew, Savannah thought fondly. She needed this time with him probably even more than he needed to be reminded that he'd shirked his "duties" as a husband.

"You can turn that off now, Cruz, I'm ready." Standing on the other side of the bed, she waited for him to comply and turn around.

She waited some more.

"Cruz?"

He made no reply.

Disappointment dropped over her like a dripping wet towel as she rounded the bed. Standing between Cruz and the television, she saw that his eyes were closed. He was breathing evenly.

He was asleep.

She pressed her lips together. Leaning over, she placed her hand on his shoulder and shook him.

Nothing. She tried harder, and still there was no response.

He was completely dead to the world.

And to her.

Short of jumping up and down on him, she thought, there was no waking him tonight.

A ragged sigh broke free as she turned off the television and then walked back into the bathroom to change. This time she put on a nightgown that had seen more than its share of sleep.

As she left the room, she looked over her shoulder one last time, hoping to find him stirring. But Cruz continued sleeping.

Fighting back tears, she went downstairs to clear the table.

Five

"I fell asleep last night, didn't I?"

Cruz's voice surprised Savannah as she walked into the kitchen the next morning.

She hadn't expected to find him home, nursing a cup of coffee at the table. Most days, he was gone by the time she got up. When she'd woken this morning to find the space next to her empty, she'd just assumed that it was business as usual for her husband.

The fact that it was, that he'd just shrugged off what had happened last night—or not happened, as the case was—had hurt. But she was getting accustomed to that.

"Yes," Savannah replied quietly as she crossed to the stove, "you did." She'd promised herself that she wasn't going to say anything, because doing so never changed things. But the words refused to remain held captive by common sense. Turning from the cabinet, a pot in her hand, she added, "Just like you have every other night in the last, oh, I don't know, maybe three months now. Maybe longer."

The apology Cruz was about to stumble through disappeared as he frowned. The last three months had been busier than usual. As his wife and his bookkeeper, she knew that.

"Look," he said, trying to hold in his temper, "it's not my fault that the mare died giving birth and that I had to play mother to her colt." That had been just one added chore on top of all the others. The herd he owned was far from large. It only numbered twenty-five, but each horse required a great deal of work. Combined, they took up his day. "It takes a lot to run a ranch. I thought you understood that."

Hurt turned to anger and Savannah struggled to rein it in. She held her tongue so as to not say something that would cause irreparable damage to a situation already tottering dangerously.

"Yes, I understood that. I understand a lot of things, Cruz." She enunciated each word carefully. "Like if we don't work at this marriage, it's not going to make it."

Marriages didn't take work, Cruz thought. They were what you sought shelter in *from* work. His parents had done that. Marriage was what was supposed to keep you sane in a world that often overwhelmed you. "What are you talking about?" he demanded.

Savannah put the pot down on the stove a little too hard. The noise reverberated through the kitchen. "Us, Cruz. I'm talking about us." She felt a sob hitch in her throat. With effort, she did her best to keep it down. "Except that there is no 'us' anymore, there's just Luke and me, and you and the ranch."

Cruz never could understand the drama that overtook women. He was sorry he'd fallen asleep last night. He'd really wanted to be with her. But she was making far too much of the incident. After all, he hadn't done it on purpose. He was just tired. "You're talking crazy, Savannah."

His accusation stung. Eyes blazing, Savannah planted her fists on her hips, fighting a strong urge to take a swing at him.

What was happening to her? She felt as if she was falling apart. "Am I? Well, maybe that's what single wives do."

"Single wives?" Now she really was talking crazy. "What the hell is that?"

"Women who are married but never see their husbands." She glared at him accusingly. "Me, Cruz, me."

He spread his hands, at a complete loss how to deal with this. "Never see their husbands? Then what is this?" He gestured to himself.

She threw up her own hands in exasperation. "A hologram for all I know. Someone who stops to have a piece of toast in the morning before leaving and comes home at night too tired to talk, too tired to spend time with me or with Luke."

They'd danced to this tune before. He didn't have time for it. "I said I'll make it up to you. To both of you." He took a breath, trying again. He hadn't waited here just for her to argue. He'd wanted to clear the air, not pollute it with anger. "Just wait until things slow up a little. I'm good for it."

Savannah laughed shortly, shaking her head. And where had she heard that before?

"At the moment you're so far in arrears, you'd have to spend every waking minute with us from now until Christmas to make up for all the lost time. Oh, wait, that's not possible because as soon as you're awake, you're outside with your horses."

She looked at him, angry tears threatening to fall. Desperate to regain her footing in his life, to have things the way they were before they began to fall apart, she moved toward him.

"If it was a woman, Cruz, I'd know what to do. I'd find a way to compete with her. But I can't compete with a ranch, with a dream. I don't know how."

As subtly as he could, he glanced at his watch. He was already late. He'd hung around in the hopes that she'd come down so that he could apologize to her. That obviously wasn't going too well.

He'd certainly had better ideas, Cruz decided, upbraiding himself.

Women had always been a mystery to him. They were soft and accommodating, and he'd sought pleasure in them while giving them pleasure. For him, that was enough— until he'd fallen for Savannah.

They'd been so in sync before. He didn't know how their relationship had become so unraveled.

"There is no competition, Savannah," he assured her. "You always come first. You and Luke. It's just that if I slack off, we're going to fall behind. Bankers and all the people who expect to be paid every month don't like excuses."

"After a while, neither do I."

He sighed, at the end of his rope. He wanted the woman he'd married to emerge again, instead of this woman who only found fault with him.

"C'mon, Savannah, I'm counting on you to be in my corner. This is for us, for Luke." He brushed a quick kiss against her cheek and picked up his hat from the table, where he'd placed it. "I promise it's not always going to be like this."

No, she thought as she watched him leave the room, *it's going to be worse.*

She'd heard this promise before, and it always *had* gotten worse. Because Cruz did not know how to delegate, how to let go.

Unless he was forced to.

With a sigh, she dragged her hand through her hair. She might as well get ready to go pick up Luke.

The doorbell rang just as Vanessa had picked up her purse and gotten her car keys out. She paused for a second. As far as she knew, she wasn't expecting anyone this afternoon.

She was on her way to Savannah's for an impromptu visit. Nothing had been arranged, but theirs was a friendship that allowed them to drop over casually.

Not that there had been very much of that taking place in the last few months. It was as if, with the advent of her second pregnancy, Savannah had crawled into herself.

Vanessa was worried about her best friend. Savannah had been looking pale lately. Pale and sad. That was one of the reasons behind her visit. If the woman was hitting a rough patch with Cruz, the least she could do was give her a shoulder to cry on.

And a few hours of peace by taking Luke off her hands wouldn't exactly hurt, either.

There was a new children's movie opening up today at the Red Rock Multiplex, and although the thought of sitting in a crowded theater with a slew of kids wasn't overly appealing to her, helping Savannah was.

Besides, she loved Luke.

Even so, she had to admit she didn't know how Savannah managed it. The boy was into absolutely everything. Exploring, taking things apart on purpose, asking an endless amount of questions. Fearless as he was, the little boy had made her heart stop on several occasions with his exploits. She could just imagine what Savannah had to be going through, putting up with this kind of thing on a daily basis.

If she had Luke 24-7 she wasn't all that sure she could survive. Savannah had a great deal more inner fortitude than she.

Murmuring "Just a minute," Vanessa swung open the door. The smile on her perfectly made up face froze.

Standing on her threshold were Gabe Thunderhawk, a local policeman, and Andrea Matthews, a detective who, in Vanessa's opinion, thought too highly of herself. What were they doing here?

It wasn't that she didn't like Gabe; she did. The policeman was an amiable man who had slipped into the post effortlessly, despite some prejudice against him from some of the older citizens because of his Native American heritage. But none of her family saw him that way. Gabe was extremely well suited to his job and, unlike some, he hadn't allowed his position to fill his head with false delusions of grandeur and power.

Ordinarily, there wasn't all that much for a local police officer to do in a town the size of Red Rock. Mostly he or one of his other two counterparts would settle a few domestic disputes, mediate over claims that A had taken something from B, be it a horse or a head of cattle or a sheep, always by "mistake."

The only real bit of excitement had happened last summer when he'd been the one to find Sarah Jenkins. The eighty-seven-year-old had wandered away from her home in the middle of the night. Somehow, the woman had managed to get beyond the town limits and, judging from the direction she'd taken, was on her way to San Antonio—barefoot and in her nightgown. Gabe had spent all night and part of the next day looking for her, tracking her the way his ancestors had once tracked their supper.

But this wasn't about anything that could make an interesting, amusing anecdote to be shared with friends on a warm night over a cold drink. This was something entirely different.

The town of Red Rock and its citizens had themselves a genuine, honest-to-goodness dead body. One courtesy of Lake Mondo, which had washed the body up onto the bank. According to the papers, the body had been in the lake for three days.

So far all they knew was that it wasn't one of the locals. No one was missing. The identity of the corpse was still a mystery. Who had killed him was a bigger one.

Without leads, both Gabe, who'd been the first on the scene, and Andrea, who was the primary on the case, had struck up a temporary, albeit uneasy alliance. Gabe didn't like taking orders from women. Andrea didn't like men who thought themselves too good to take orders from women. It wasn't a match made in heaven.

Determined to get one up on the other, they had worked hard, dug deep, looking for some kind of link or starting point. Because of the unusual birthmark they'd found on the body, they had temporarily connected the dead man to Vanessa's father, a fact that made her furious. Everyone knew Ryan Fortune was a pillar of the community.

They had already dragged him out to the lake and fired questions at him, as if they could get him to admit to something by overwhelming him with inquiries.

Vanessa viewed both people on her doorstep with less than friendly regard. She held the door ajar, when normally she would have thrown it open and welcomed in at least Gabe, whom she knew better. Andrea had always been reserved, a woman with something to prove. Vanessa found she couldn't relate to her. They moved in different circles.

"Hello, Gabe. Detective Matthews." She nodded at both, her hand remaining on the door, barring both of them from entering.

Gabe looked slightly uncomfortable about the reason that had brought him and one of Red Rock's top detectives there. The Fortunes were not people to come up against lightly, and that was just what he was doing. Confident in his abilities and determined to one day make the grade as a detective himself, the twenty-nine-year-old police officer had no trouble fitting into the world of the white man, as his grandfather still referred to anyone outside of their tribe.

Gabe glanced at the purse and keys in Vanessa's hand. "Going somewhere?"

"Yes, as a matter-of-fact, I am." She looked toward her car in the driveway. "And I'm running late." The last was a lie, but she didn't feel like having to put up with what she thought was ahead.

"We won't keep you long," Andrea told her crisply. She looked over Vanessa's shoulder into the house. "Mind if we come in?" It wasn't really a question, Vanessa knew.

In so many words, Andrea was telling her she wanted them to be admitted.

Vanessa bit back the "yes, I do mind" that was hovering on her lips, but she didn't bother suppressing a sigh as she stepped back and opened the door.

Andrea walked in first, followed by Gabe, who flashed an apologetic smile at her as he crossed the threshold.

By nature Vanessa was outgoing and cooperative. She was also extremely protective of those she loved, and this investigation, for some unfair reason, seemed to be targeting her father, a man who wouldn't have hurt a fly unless that fly was totting a six-shooter aimed directly at him. And even then he'd try to disarm the fly first.

Her eyes narrowed as she regarded the two interlopers, neither of whom had ever been inside her house before. "What can I do for you?"

Gabe got down to it. He didn't know any other way. "Has your father been acting strangely lately?"

Her first instinct was to voice a denial. The problem was, however, that Gabe's question did have some merit. Her father *had* been acting strangely of late. He'd been unusually closemouthed for a while now. So much so that she and her siblings were concerned that something might be wrong.

Their speculation in no way pointed toward the ludicrous idea of murder. They thought that perhaps his marriage to Lily, his third wife, who had coincidentally also been his childhood sweetheart, wasn't working out for some reason, causing their father pain and concern.

Sometimes, she knew, the dream was better than reality.

But she wasn't about to give Gabe or the curly-haired

brunette he was with anything to work with. If for some reason her father's marriage wasn't working out, it was none of their business.

"My father has been acting like my father. There's nothing strange about his behavior." Her tone indicated that she considered the subject closed.

She might have, but apparently Andrea didn't. The woman took a small notepad out of her jacket pocket and referred to notes she'd taken earlier.

"Some of the people who work for him say he's been acting preoccupied lately. Distant."

Vanessa lifted her head, a tigress ready to defend her cub.

"My father is in charge of a great many things. At times, it's hard keeping everything straight. Especially when you want to give a hundred and ten percent of yourself in all aspects." She looked at Gabe to back her up, since in her judgment he'd be more acquainted with Ryan Fortune's dealings than the aloof Matthews. "If he's guilty of anything, it's working too hard and being too generous." Her eyes narrowed as she looked at Andrea. "I can supply you with a list of charity foundations he either heads or is on the board of, if you like."

"That won't be necessary," the detective told her tersely. "We're not looking for contributions, only answers."

Taking a cue from the words, Vanessa drew herself up. "Do you have anything specific to ask me, Detective Matthews?"

"No." Gabe cut in before Andrea could answer. Right now, they were merely on a fishing trip, trying to get a feel for things. They were still looking into reports filed on missing persons and if any of those had unusual birthmarks. It wouldn't do to demand a verification of the town's richest and most well-respected man's whereabouts and dealings for the last two months.

Andrea glared at him, but made no contradiction. That surprised him.

"All right, Gabe." Vanessa deliberately ignored the other woman in the room. "Why don't you get back to me when you do? Until then…"

Gabe knew Andrea was annoyed by the snub. Stepping closer to Vanessa, she took out a four-by-five photograph of the corpse. There wasn't much to recognize, but the birthmark that had been discovered above the man's right buttock had been digitally enhanced. She held it up for Vanessa to view. "Do you recognize this birthmark?"

Vanessa had no desire to look at a body that had been submerged until hardly anything of him had been left to recognize. As she struggled with her anger, her eyes locked with Andrea's.

"You already have the answer to that or you wouldn't be here in my house, asking not too subtle questions about my father. Do I have a missing relative who had one of those birthmarks? No. Do I have an idea who this person is? Again, no. And it goes without saying that I wouldn't know who would want to kill him." She spared a glance toward Gabe. "Or if he even was killed. Maybe he fell off a boat somewhere, drowned and wound up washing ashore here." To her, it was as good a theory as any.

"He might have fallen off a boat," Andrea informed her tersely, putting the photograph away again, "but he didn't drown. He was shot first."

Vanessa had had just about enough of this. "My father

doesn't shoot people. My family doesn't shoot people—even when we're sorely tempted."

"Vanessa." There was a warning note in Gabe's stern voice.

She flashed him a tight smile. "Sorry, I'm not at my best with veiled accusations of murder thrown at the people I love." Her hand tightened around the keys she'd never put away. "Now if you'll excuse me, I was, as you so expertly noticed—" she aimed the words at Andrea "—on my way out when you rang the doorbell."

After a moment the woman turned and walked to the front door. But Gabe hung back a few steps. His eyes met Vanessa's.

"I'm just doing my job," he told her.

"I know." Opening the door, she allowed the detective out and watched her as she walked across the driveway to their car. "Too bad you can't get to pick your helpers in this case."

She saw a hint of a smile on Gabe's otherwise stoic features. It was easy to see that he didn't disagree with her.

Less than half an hour later, Vanessa brought her car to a halt in front of Savannah and Cruz's house. She was still stewing about Gabe and Andrea's visit as she got out. How could they possibly think her father had anything to do with the dead man? As straight as an arrow, he'd be the first one at the sheriff's office if he even remotely knew anything. Not only that, but he'd call a family meeting to inform them.

Since no such meeting had been called, she was confident that it was just some freak accident of nature that someone bearing the same birthmark as her father had washed up on their shores.

Truth was always stranger than fiction, right?

Raising her hand to knock on the front door, she heard a crash and a scream. Both came from inside the house.

Not standing on ceremony, Vanessa quickly turned the knob, opening the door. Her heart was in her throat as she surveyed the living room.

Her eyes riveted directly on Luke. Her godson had a frayed beige towel tucked into the back neckline of his shirt, like a cape. His feet were on the floor and his body was surrounded by a coffee table. The one that had, until five seconds ago, a glass top.

He appeared unharmed and definitely not as upset as his mother. It was obvious that he had gone through the table while executing some complicated flying maneuver in his alter ego as a superhero.

Savannah looked as if she was about to break into as many pieces as there were glass shards on the floor.

Rushing in, Vanessa pulled out her cell phone. "Do you want me to call for the paramedics?"

"Aunt 'Nessa!" Luke exclaimed with glee, apparently completely unmindful of what he'd just done and how close he'd come to slicing himself open in over a dozen places. The boy started to turn toward her.

Savannah grabbed his shoulders, holding him in place. "Stay still," she ordered. One wrong move on his part and his legs would wind up being lacerated from all sides.

Her heart pounding in her chest, Savannah took a quick inventory of the situation. As fantastic as it seemed, it looked as if, so far, Luke was completely unscathed by his newest adventure. She sighed. She needed eyes in the back of her head with this boy.

Vanessa had rushed to the child's side. "Listen to your

mother, Luke, and keep very still." Biting her lower lip, she looked at Savannah, almost afraid to ask. "How bad is it?"

"The kid has a charmed life," Savannah said. "I don't see any cuts." Unable to remain inert for more than the count of two, Luke began to move again. "Stay perfectly still, Luke," she repeated, then added, "like a statue," for good measure.

His dark eyes were dancing. "What kind of statue, Mama?"

"The kind that doesn't move," she told him, barely managing not to snap at him. Her nerves were far more frayed than the edges of the towel her son had appropriated for his makeshift costume. Very carefully, she removed the remaining shards of glass from the coffee table top.

In an attempt to keep Luke's attention from what Savannah was doing, Vanessa told him, "I'm going to take you to the movies."

"The movies?" the boy cried excitedly.

"But only if you listen to your mother and don't move," Vanessa cautioned, afraid he was going to start wiggling again. "She needs to get you out of there."

"I'm Super Jake." His small fisted hand thumped against his equally small chest. "I can get myself out."

"Not without a lot of blood," Savannah warned, removing another piece of glass and placing it on top of the book she was using to collect all the shards.

He tossed his head the way Vanessa had often seen Savannah do. "Doesn't scare me."

"Sure scares me," Vanessa told him as she kept one eye on the boy and one on Savannah and the progress she was making.

A magnanimous look came over the boy's features. "Okay. For you, Aunt 'Nessa, I'll stay still."

"Done," Savannah finally said several minutes later, putting the last piece of glass on top of the pile she'd collected. There was now a glaring hole where the top of her coffee table had once been.

Vanessa closed her arms around the boy and lifted him up, careful to avoid touching what was left of the jagged sides.

Ticklish, he laughed and hugged her.

Once she was certain that her son wasn't bleeding, Savannah collapsed on the sofa. "Remind me never to go through that again."

"Okay, Mama," Luke said innocently. So innocently that all she could do was laugh.

"You don't have to take him, you know," she said to Vanessa.

"Sure I do. That's why I came over. That and to ask you to a wedding."

Savannah sat up. "Whose?"

"My cousin Steve's. He's marrying Amy Burke-Sinclair in the fall. I wanted to give you a heads-up and tell you that, naturally, you and Cruz are invited."

Luke turned up his face toward her like a sunflower tracking the sun. "How about me?"

Vanessa pretended to think the question over. "Only if you promise not to leap into the wedding cake—or anything else, for that matter."

Laughing, Luke hugged her. "I promise."

A wedding, Savannah thought, utterly drained. Something to look forward to. If she was still married to Cruz come the fall.

Six

After getting him a change of clothing and carefully examining Luke one last time, Savannah allowed her son to go play a video game in the family room.

Coming back into the living room, she saw that Vanessa had already collected the larger pieces of glass from the floor and was now taking the vacuum cleaner from the hall closet to give the area a thorough once-over.

They didn't make any better friends than that, Savannah thought as she put her hand over Vanessa's and took the vacuum cleaner with a smile. "I'll do that."

Vanessa glanced toward the other room. "Luke's okay?"

"Like it never happened."

The resiliency of her son never ceased to amaze Savannah. She used to be like that, she thought. Until life had conspired to overwhelm her. Taking a deep breath, she gave the entire area a slow, thorough vacuuming.

As she turned off the machine, she felt a new surge of energy come from nowhere. Savannah used it to give her the wherewithal to make a decision. Life was not going to overwhelm her. She was going to overwhelm it. Or die in the process.

"I'd love to come," Savannah suddenly said to Vanessa as she gathered up the cord and tucked it around the machine. "To the wedding," she clarified when her friend looked at her quizzically.

Vanessa opened the closet door so Savannah could return the vacuum to its place. "You, singular, not you, plural?"

She glanced toward the next room to see if Luke was listening, but the boy was completely captivated by the video game he was playing. She hoped that lasted more than ten minutes.

"These days, I really don't feel that I can speak for Cruz."

Closing the closet door, Vanessa followed Savannah back into the living room. "Want to talk about it?"

Savannah thought about last night and how disappointed she'd felt when she'd walked out of the bathroom and found Cruz sound asleep.

"No, it'll only depress me." She bit her lip, torn between loyalty to her husband and the need to talk to someone she knew and trusted. Someone who would be sympathetic. "But I really feel as if the fairy tale was just that, a fairy tale." A rueful smile curved her mouth. "I'm beginning to understand why the stories always end after the prince and princess get together. If it followed them beyond that vague 'and they lived happily ever after,' if it *showed* you how they lived, then everybody would really be disappointed."

Vanessa tried to read between the lines. She and Devin had been married a little longer than Savannah and Cruz. She knew the dangers of complacency, of having a routine slowly turn into a rut. "You need to shake things up."

Savannah laughed softly, shaking her head. "I've thought about shaking him…" And then she stopped, realizing that Vanessa might get an unfair picture of the way Cruz was. It wasn't as if he was doing this to spite her. She knew he was doing the best he could. They were both stuck on this insane merry-go-round that life had flung them onto. She just had no idea how to slow things down. "But how can I really fault him? He's working hard at trying to make the ranch into something. It's not as if he's out all hours of the night with other women."

Vanessa was quick to agree. "You've got a good guy, Savannah."

Savannah smiled. She supposed that was what she liked best about Vanessa. Her friend didn't take sides, wasn't critical of Cruz; she just listened. "I know." She sighed, dragging her hand through her hair in a helpless gesture. "Just not an attentive one."

Luke squealed in the background and Vanessa glanced toward the boy. Just keeping after him was a full-time job. Even when you loved a child, that could be extremely wearing.

"He might be attentive if you got him away from all the distractions."

Her own attention taken up by Luke, Savannah looked at her quizzically. "What do you mean?"

Vanessa smiled, leaning toward her friend as if she was imparting some age-old, well-kept secret. "Get away."

As if it was that easy. "We don't have the time or money for a vacation right now."

And by the time they could take one, who knew if they'd even be on speaking terms? she thought. Things just kept escalating between them every time she tried to fix them.

Vanessa was shaking her own head. "I'm not talking about a two-week vacation, Savannah, I'm talking about taking a couple of days. Go someplace for the weekend. The two of you never really had that much time alone. Luke was born after you were married for three months. You two deserve some alone time." She glanced to where Luke was cheering his victory over two racers. "I can take Luke. He thinks that Devin's a great guy and it lets Devin practice his parenting skills. It'd be a treat for everyone all around. C'mon, say yes."

Vanessa made it sound as if it would be a treat for her, Savannah thought, instead of for Cruz and herself. Still, as much as she wanted to, Savannah knew she couldn't automatically agree. "I can't say yes for Cruz."

He friend slipped her arm around her shoulders. "No, but you can make him want to say yes. Look, I knew Cruz before you did. I know what a so-called 'bad boy' he was. He had women trailing after him wherever he went. I can remember one actually hiring him to help her with her horse. He did it after hours." An amused smile curved Vanessa's lips. "Did her after hours, too, most likely. She made no bones about the fact that she lusted after his fine Latin hide."

Savannah could well understand women being attracted to Cruz. She could also understand what being viewed as nothing more than just a stud rather than a complete person could do to Cruz's self-esteem. Maybe that was why he worked so hard at making the ranch a success.

"That's awful."

"Yes, it's awful," Vanessa readily agreed. "I think even though he was flattered and enjoyed himself, he resented it a little. Maybe more than a little." And then she confirmed what Savannah had suspected. "To the women who wanted him, Cruz was hardly more than a handsome trophy, a prize they wanted to snag for the thrill of it." She looked at Savannah pointedly. "He took what they offered and had a good time. I didn't think he was ever going to settle down and get married. Why do you think Rosita adores you so much?"

Savannah shrugged. She'd never given it much thought. "Because I love her son?"

Vanessa smiled at her friend's sweet naiveté. "Because you *changed* her son. Changed him from a swaggering Romeo to a decent man his family could be proud of. They loved him before you came along, but they only *liked* him after you came into his life. You worked a miracle with that man, Savannah. Whether you know it or not, it was nothing short of a miracle."

An amused smile played on Savannah's lips. As far as she was concerned, no miracles had transpired. Once he knew the child she was carrying was his, Cruz had worked hard at convincing her to marry him. She hadn't done anything except love him. "Aren't you exaggerating just a little?"

Vanessa's right eyebrow rose a little higher as she looked at her friend. "Am I? He changed the way he was because he loved you. Gave up his loose, tomcat ways to make himself into a man you could love."

He didn't have to change for that to happen. "I loved him the first minute I saw him."

Vanessa held up her finger, making her point. "But he didn't know that. I think that all Cruz really knew about was the physical side of love, the red-hot attraction that takes place. And he was living proof that that kind of thing doesn't last, not on its own. He wanted what was between the two of you to last."

She looked at Savannah intently. She just *knew* her friend's marriage could be salvaged—and made stronger for the test.

"Work with that, Savannah. Make Cruz remember why he's laboring so hard out there from sunup to sundown—"

"Longer," Savannah interjected.

"Okay, longer." She could see the hesitation in Savannah's eyes, as if this was a last-ditch effort and if it didn't work, then nothing would. As long as she could cling to it, as long as she had this to still turn to, then she had hope. If this failed, there'd be nothing left to hang on to. "If you ask him to go, he won't say no."

Savannah laughed. "He says no to me in a million ways now."

"Silently," Vanessa pointed out. "I guarantee that if you put it to him, if you tell him how much this weekend getaway means to you, that you want to reaffirm your feelings for each other without any demands on your time but each other, he won't turn you down."

Savannah chewed on her lower lip. Vanessa sounded a great deal more certain about the matter than she felt. "You're that sure?"

"I'm that sure. Like I said, I was there in the very beginning. I got to see the difference in Cruz, you didn't." It had done her heart good to see Cruz fall in love the way he had. Aside from a three-week crush she'd had on him as an adolescent, she'd always regarded him as a brother. "That man would walk on hot coals for you."

"I don't want him to walk on hot coals. I just want him to make hot love to me."

"Even better." Vanessa laughed, giving her a hug. "That's my girl."

The idea began to take on depth and breadth. Savannah did a quick mental inventory of their closets. She looked at Vanessa ruefully. Of the two of them, Vanessa had been the one who had gone places, seen things. She had always been strictly a homebody. "I'm not even sure where our suitcases are."

Vanessa looked at her innocently. "What do you need suitcases for?"

"The hotel might not like us bringing our clothes in grocery bags."

"What do you need clothes for?" Vanessa countered. Unable to suppress it any longer, she grinned broadly. "Spend the weekend naked."

Savannah glanced over to see if Luke was listening, but the boy was still playing the video game and mercifully oblivious to his surroundings.

Savannah lowered her voice. "I couldn't—"

"Yes, you could," Vanessa insisted. "And that's what this is all about. Being with each other. Clothing shouldn't be optional, it should be banned." She underscored her statement with a wink. "Trust me."

As Savannah thought about it, the idea began to take on merit. After all, this was probably going to be the last time they would be alone together. It wouldn't be long before their family would swell to four.

"He'll wonder what's come over me," she said, although she wasn't really protesting very much.

Vanessa squeezed her hand. "And he'll be thrilled to death." She gave her friend's form a quick once-over. "Five months pregnant and there isn't an ounce of extra fat on you. You're just as beautiful as the first time Cruz saw you. Use that, Savannah. Use it to your advantage."

Savannah glanced down at herself. Other than trying to look neat and not haggard, she hadn't given her appearance all that much thought lately, except for last night, of course. Maybe that was part of the problem. "You think?"

Vanessa nodded. "I think."

A warmth began to travel through Savannah as she envisioned herself alone with her husband. As she envisioned the two of them the way they once were, before the world and Cruz's goals intruded. "I'm getting excited."

Vanessa laughed. "Well, don't do it with me. Save it for Cruz."

Overwhelmed with gratitude and with her hope renewed, Savannah threw her arms around her friend. "You're the best, Vanessa."

Vanessa returned the embrace, happy to have brought a smile back to Savannah's face. "That's what I keep telling Devin."

Luke chose that moment to make it a group hug. "Me, too!" he announced loudly, bouncing onto the sofa next to his mother.

"Yes," Savannah laughed, dragging him onto her lap, "you, too."

She gave him a huge heartfelt hug. Things, she promised herself, were going to work out. She was in love with her baby's father and he was a good man. How could they not work out?

Instead of flying by on its magic carpet the way every day seemed to lately, the day felt as if it was comprised of endless minutes knitting themselves into endless hours. She could have sworn that she'd been waiting for Cruz to come home forever.

Savannah knew exactly where he was. At the corral, training the new horses. He was at the point where he would separate one from the others, taking it aside for intensified sessions. She didn't have to saddle up to reach him, just walk a ways.

But she knew how he was when he was working. It required all of his concentration. He wouldn't be in the best of moods if she interrupted and asked him to call it a night. Barring some sort of emergency, that was his decision to make, not hers.

Doing the right thing could get taxing at times, she thought, fighting back frustration as she stared at the front door and willed it to open.

When Cruz finally did walk into the house, it was close to eight. The sun was receding, taking daylight with it and leaving the land to slumber for a short while.

The familiar sound of his boots outside the front door as he stomped off the dirt had her hurrying to admit him.

Cruz looked surprised to have her opening the door for him. "Such service," he murmured affectionately as he pressed a kiss to her forehead.

The sigh he released died abruptly as he saw the coffee table. Stunned, he stared at it for a moment. The table had been an indulgence, since it required constant upkeep. Savannah was forever cleaning fingerprints off it. Even so, he knew how much she loved it.

The glass had all been cleared away, but there was no ignoring the large gaping hole where it had once been.

He looked at her over his shoulder. "That's a new look," he commented dryly. "What happened?"

"Luke discovered he couldn't fly." She saw Cruz's eyebrows raise in silent query for more information. "He tried to take off from the sofa."

His eyes immediately looked up to the boy's room. "Is he hurt?"

She shook her head, taking the lead toward the dining room. "Luckily, no."

"You've got to keep a closer eye on him."

She didn't take kindly to the implication that she was lax in her parenting duties, even from Cruz. "The only way my eye would be any closer is if I put Luke in a cage and stared at him all day from a foot away. He's just too high-spirited."

"No such thing." And then Cruz grinned as he thought back to his own childhood. "My mother'll tell you I was like that as a kid."

Savannah placed a casserole dish in the center of the table and then regarded him for a moment. He appeared none the worse for wear. "You mean there's hope?"

"There's always hope." The grin melted into a smile. She had her hands full, he thought. Just as his mother had. Except in his mother's case, there had been five of them, not just one, and she'd worked full-time for the Fortunes, as well. "I'll talk to him." Talking was not his long suit. Actions did the speaking for him. Maybe it was time to introduce the boy into the family business. "Maybe I'll take him with me tomorrow."

Savannah thought of how caught up with his work Cruz got. How the other hands would be busy with the myriad things it took to run this ranch. Those were perfect conditions for an accident waiting to happen. "No."

He looked at her sharply. She'd never opposed him before. "What do you mean, no?"

"I mean no, it's not a good idea to take Luke with you when you work. Not yet, anyway. He's at an age where he requires full-time attention, Cruz. You'll be too busy to watch him every moment. Luke gets into trouble here and I'm on him almost constantly. Out there, who knows?"

He supposed she made sense. Still, there would be consequences if they handled the boy with kid gloves, watching his every step.

Cruz helped himself to some of the casserole. "I don't want my son growing up to be a wimp."

"He won't be a wimp," she promised. "He'll be alive."

Cruz snorted, taking a healthy forkful of food. "Seems to me that I can't do a much worse job." He bit his lower lip the moment the words were out. That sounded critical and he hadn't meant to be. He was just too tired to function. "I didn't mean that."

"Yes, you did."

Savannah was hurt, and it was on the tip of her tongue to retaliate. To say that she thought they needed a break from each other for a while. Part of her still believed that, despite all her plans to keep them together, their marriage was in serious trouble.

But she just couldn't say that to Cruz. She knew once the words were out, there would be no turning back. She couldn't say for sure how Cruz would react, but she knew the assessment would badly wound his pride. And ultimately, that was where he lived—in his pride. Any kind of temporary break might turn into a permanent one. She didn't want that. She couldn't imagine her life without Cruz.

Sitting down opposite him, she reached across the table and placed her hand on his. She wanted his undivided attention. "We need to get away."

A small hissing sound came from between his teeth. "Look, if this is about last night—"

"Yes, it's about last night." She couldn't very well deny that. But it was about more than that. "And all the other nights that came before."

He looked at her indignantly. "It hasn't been all bad," he said defensively.

She didn't want this getting off on the wrong foot. "I'm not saying that."

His dark eyes narrowed as he began to eat again. "So what *are* you saying?"

She struggled not to get emotional, knowing that if she did, she'd lose the advantage, not to mention his attention.

"I'm saying that lately we're both too tired to enjoy each other. That we're both working at maximum capacity and that we're running out of steam in the areas that really count." She looked at him pointedly. "I don't want us to grow apart."

He took her comment the only way he knew how. "And I do?"

She knew that defensive tone, knew that she could easily get sucked into an argument, but that wasn't what she was after. What she wanted was a resolution.

"I don't think so," Savannah told him. "It's what I'm banking on." She reached across the table again and took his hand in hers in mute supplication. "Let's get away, Cruz."

"You mean run away?"

She liked the sound of that, she decided. "Yes. Run away," she repeated. "For the weekend, let's just run away." Her voice picked up speed as she tried to get him to come on board. "Let's go to San Antonio, rent a nice hotel room, stay in bed and make love the whole two days."

Weary from the day's chores, he forced a smile to his lips. "We don't have to go away to do that, Savannah. We could do it here."

She knew better and so did he, she thought. "The point is, we *haven't* done that here. If we stay at home, weekend or weekday, there are just too many distractions, too many demands on your time and on mine. If we go away, then there's nothing for us to concentrate on except each other."

He frowned, not liking what he was hearing. "You could just walk off and leave Luke?"

Why was he fighting her on this? "You make it sound as if I was going to leave him standing waist deep in a water trough with buzzards circling around his head. Vanessa's offered to take him for the weekend." She threw in the clincher. "And he'd get back a rested mother at the end of this."

"Vanessa," he said slowly, the light dawning. "Is this her idea?"

Savannah watched his eyes for signs of anger as she said, "Yes."

Suspicion darkened his brow. He never discussed their private life with anyone, not even members of his family. "Have you been complaining to her about our love life?"

Now there was a laugh. She withdrew her hand. "What love life?"

His eyes darkened ominously. He liked Vanessa, but what happened—or didn't happen—between his wife and him behind closed doors was his business, not hers. "Is that what you said?"

He was focusing on the wrong thing, damn it. Didn't he see that? "She's my closest friend. With close friends, you don't have to voice everything. You just know things about each other. Besides, this isn't about your machismo," she insisted, "this is about us. About being together." She looked at him, suddenly afraid of what she would discover. "Don't you want to be alone with me?"

"Sure I do." How could she even think that? "But everything I do is for you."

She thought if she heard that one more time, she was going to scream. That she didn't scream was a huge display of self-control, and she silently congratulated herself for it.

"Then do this one more thing for me," she begged. "Take the weekend off. The hands know how to take care of the horses for two days. Tell Hank or Billy or Jaime that you're taking off with your wife because if you don't do it soon, you'll forget what she looks like."

His expression softened as he looked at her for the first time that evening. Really looked at her.

"Never happen. Your image is etched right here." He pointed to his heart.

And was that enough for him? she wondered. After five years, was he satisfied with just that and nothing more substantial? "Is that your way of saying that we're not going?"

"No, that's my way of saying that no matter how busy I get, I don't stop loving you." He took a breath, considering the matter again. What she was asking for wasn't that unreasonable. And maybe he could stand to be away from his work for a while. Maybe it would even do him some good. "Okay, make a reservation and tell Vanessa she's got a new man in her life."

Rising from the table, Savannah circled to where he was sitting and threw her arms around his neck. "Thank you."

Cruz laughed as he pulled his wife onto his lap and kissed her soundly. "You're welcome. Now, if you don't let me eat, I'm not going to have strength left for that weekend."

Her eyes dancing, she slid off his lap and began to fill up his plate again. "Then by all means, eat."

Seven

"You sure Vanessa's up to taking Luke in?" Cruz asked the following morning.

Standing at the stove, Savannah stiffened slightly. Here it came, she thought, the disclaimer. He was looking for a way to back out of this.

She'd forced herself out of bed the moment she'd felt Cruz stirring, determined to prepare breakfast for him. Determined to try to make a new start from this moment on, since he was making an effort to do the same by agreeing to go away for the weekend with her.

Happily, she hadn't felt the urge to go running into the bathroom first thing this morning. But that didn't mean she felt up to par. The truth was, she was so far from it that she was barely at the beginning of the tee.

Still, she'd vowed to be the cheerful, loving wife this morning or die in the attempt.

But she didn't like the way this conversation seemed to be going.

She forced herself to pay attention to the eggs she was making. Flipping them over, she asked as calmly as she could, "Why wouldn't she be up to it?"

Cruz sipped his coffee. "Because of the rumors."

The toast popped. She buttered it quickly, placing it on the plate. "What rumors?"

He watched Savannah slide the eggs out of the pan onto the plate, then bring it over to the table. She wasn't eating anything herself, he noticed. Was she still feeling sick?

"They say the body they found at the lake is somehow connected to Ryan. Maybe even a long-lost illegitimate son, finally coming forward after all these years. Why aren't you eating anything?"

"Not hungry." She glanced down at the cup of tea on the table in front of her. "What else are they saying?"

"That maybe the guy was going to expose Ryan if he didn't come through with a sizable chunk of the Fortune empire as hush money." Cruz couldn't help wondering if it was true. If all those years of respectability had been an attempt to bury the man Ryan Fortune really was. It wouldn't be the first time a wealthy man tried to bury his past with good deeds.

Savannah frowned at the idea. "Expose Ryan? As what?"

He knew Savannah liked the man. Hell, he liked the man. Ryan Fortune had always treated him decently. But that wouldn't change the facts if they turned out to be true.

"As being something other than the upstanding pillar of the community we all think he is."

Savannah took offense for Ryan. Not against her husband, but against the faceless people of Red Rock and beyond, the ones who lived for gossip and dirt as a way to take away the dullness of their own small, boring lives.

"Ryan *is* the man we think he is. He's kind, noble and charitable to a fault. I've never seen that man talk down to anyone. He was very kind to me when I had nowhere to turn." She'd lost her teaching position at the school because of her pregnancy and no one would hire a pregnant woman. It was Ryan who took her on to help with the accounting when he clearly didn't have to.

Cruz felt she was forgetting one important thing. After all, Ryan Fortune wasn't a saint. Nobody was. "That was because of Vanessa."

Savannah wondered if Cruz was deliberately taking the other side of the argument to start a fight so that he could call off the trip.

Struggling not to make any accusations, she approached the situation logically.

"If it was in Ryan Fortune's character to be a bastard, it would have come out way before now," she pointed out. "He's dealt with too many people to keep his true nature a secret—if that was his true nature. Which," she concluded, "it isn't."

Cruz couldn't help grinning as he ate his breakfast. "Pretty loyal, aren't you?"

Savannah raised her chin proudly. "It's one of my good points. I stick with things even when the road gets bumpy."

He heard the inflection in her voice, saw the look in her eyes as she gazed at him. It didn't take a brain surgeon to figure out what she was talking about. "Meaning me?"

"Meaning us," she corrected. And while she was at it, she shot down any attempt he might make at wiggling out of his promise because there was no one to look after their son. "And if Vanessa couldn't take Luke for some reason, there's always your mom or one of your sisters." She gave him a knowing look. "Can't use that to fall back on, mister."

"I wasn't using that to fall back on," he informed her. And then he frowned. "But…"

She braced herself, ready to shoot down anything else he came up with. They just *had* to get away. She had this feeling that if they didn't, their marriage was doomed. "'But?'"

He'd had to pay cash for the four horses. Cash against the money he hoped to collect from the man who was going to pay him once the animals had been trained to be cutting horses.

"We really don't have that much cash available." He could sense that this was important to her, so he qualified it rather than try to postpone the trip the way he'd first thought to do. "Can't be a very expensive place."

She did a little quick thinking. Compromise was the essence of survival. "It won't be," she told him brightly. "It'll be free."

"Free? Why?" The next moment, he came up with his own answer to that. This had been Vanessa's idea. What if the woman made her a gift of it? He liked the Fortunes well enough, but he wasn't about to be the object of their pity. "I won't take charity."

Savannah stared at him. She had no idea what he was talking about. "Charity?"

She knew damn well what he was talking about, Cruz thought. "If Vanessa is 'treating' us, tell your friend to put away her checkbook. A Perez always pays his own way."

So that was it. Had he always been this thin-skinned, or

was trying to develop a superranch in a record amount of time getting to him? "A Perez—and in case you've forgotten, I am one, too—doesn't have to pay his own way if there's nothing to pay."

Finished eating, he pushed his plate back. "What are you talking about?"

She'd had her heart set on going to a hotel, having their meals sent up to their room, luxuriating in a king-size bed with nothing more than the blankets, pillow and Cruz for comfort. But the one important ingredient in the scenario was Cruz; everything else was expendable. Which was why she'd done a little quick recalculating to make it more acceptable to him.

"Going camping."

"Camping?" he echoed. He ended the word with a wide smile.

One look at his face told her that she'd made the right decision. As much as he maintained that he wanted to attain the good life, to have everything the Fortunes had, there was no denying the fact that the man inside was still Cruz Perez. Someone who liked to go camping, who enjoyed getting away from everything, including the life he so zealously aspired to.

"Camping," she repeated with a smile.

"But I thought you wanted room service."

"I want your service most of all." Getting up, she crossed to him and cupped his cheek. "I figure I'd have more of a chance at that if you were happy."

It was time to go. He needed to get back to training those horses he'd bought if he was going to have them ready on time. Especially if he was going to lose two days in the bargain.

He stood up and kissed the top of Savannah's head. "You're the best."

She wanted to savor the moment, to lose herself in Cruz's arms, but she knew he had to leave. With a laugh, she threw back her head. "You're just finding that out now?"

He laughed, too, picking up his hat from the table. "No, just taking a refresher course." Putting on the Stetson, he began to walk out.

"You could start by kissing me goodbye," she called after him. "Properly," she tagged on before he could try to pass off that fleeting brushing of his lips against her hair as a kiss.

Turning on his heel, Cruz blew out a breath, as if bracing himself. "It's a dirty job, but I guess someone's got to do it."

With a laugh, she grabbed him by the lapels she'd ironed only the day before, and pulled him to her. "And that someone's you, mister." Her smile faded a little as emotion filled her throat. "And it always will be."

Cruz took her into his arms and lowered his mouth to hers.

He was in a hurry and it was only meant to be a quick, perfunctory kiss. Something to hold his place until he had more time to give himself up to the moment and the desire that was always there, just buried beneath details and minutia.

But something took hold of him the second his mouth was on hers.

Maybe it was the promise of being alone with her again, sans the myriad demands that always took his attention away. Maybe it was that he missed being with her the way it had been in the very beginning, when each day began and ended in her eyes.

He wasn't sure.

All he knew was that the taste of her lips this morning triggered something inside of him, igniting it again. That old feeling he'd once had, where he couldn't wait to see her, to be with her.

For one brief moment in time, the long years of marriage, with its routine that caused him to take things for granted, faded into the background, along with the overwhelming weight of all the responsibilities he had on his shoulders. For a brief moment, all there was was Savannah.

He sank into the kiss, allowing the fire that came up into his belly to spread out to his limbs.

Making him want her.

Making him wish with all his soul that he didn't have to walk out that door in the next few minutes because his men and his ranch were all waiting on him.

Savannah had no idea what came over her husband, or why. All she knew was that for a second, he was her Cruz again, the man who could have made her walk to the ends of the earth if he'd so much as indicated that he wanted her to.

The man who could make her head spin and her pulse race even faster than it had the moment she'd seen Luke go crashing onto the tabletop and then through it; or the time she'd seen him sail off his swing and arc into the air, only to mercifully land in his sand pile, sustaining bruises instead of broken bones.

Her pulse raced faster than all that.

Her fingers tightened around the lapels she was grasping as she rose up on her toes, sinking further into the kiss.

Into the promise.

She felt his body harden against her and she smiled broadly against his lips.

Finally, Cruz forced himself to pull back, knowing he was at the critical point. If he didn't stop now, he wasn't going to. And there was no telling when Luke would come down or one of his men might come to the door, looking for him, wondering what was keeping him.

He smiled down into her eyes. "Consider that a retainer."

Savannah grinned, touching her lips as she leaned against the table at her back. "If I knew you were going to react that way, I would have suggested camping a lot sooner."

He was about to answer her when there was a knock on the front door.

"Go." She waved him off. "That's bound to be Hank, wondering why you haven't come out to play yet."

"Play," he snorted, shaking his head. "Woman, do you have any idea what it is I do out there?"

"You work very, very hard," she agreed. "But you also like what you're doing. It's not as if you're putting on a jacket and tie and going off to sit behind a desk in an office all day." She knew that would have killed him as surely as a well-aimed bullet. There was another knock on the door and she shooed him again. "Now go. Make yourself and us proud," she instructed.

In that order, too, she thought as she watched him head out the front door. Because if Cruz wasn't proud of himself, then no amount of words from her could make him feel that way. He needed it as much as he needed the very air he breathed.

Savannah just wished it wouldn't take quite so much out of him.

* * *

They were getting worse.

Coming out of nowhere, the headaches would attack without warning, laying siege to his temples, his forehead. Wild, savage little men with pickaxes would storm over his skull and begin pounding madly.

Sometimes the headaches were almost blinding.

Sitting at his desk in his spacious office suite, Ryan Fortune ran his hand along his forehead, as if the action could somehow make the almost wrenching pain recede, if only a little.

But it didn't.

Just as he knew it wouldn't.

He sighed, telling himself it was a case of mind over matter. Telling himself to hold on until this newest bout would fade, as it always had before.

It felt as if the very top of his skull was being torn off.

The headaches were happening more frequently now, and it was getting harder and harder to pretend that nothing was wrong. That this was just some anomaly, an annoying roadblock that his body was throwing up for no apparent reason.

Aches and pains were facts of life. First they assaulted you as growing pains, then they came along in a different form because you were growing older. In every case, he'd learned that you just pushed on, not allowing yourself to be conquered.

But it was getting harder to do.

These days, Ryan found himself swallowing extra-strength aspirin by the handful. He'd no sooner open one bottle than the contents seemed to evaporate. He tried to hold out, but it wasn't possible.

Opening the middle drawer in his desk, he took out a

large bottle he'd opened just two days ago. It was less than half-full now.

Twisting off the cap, he shook out three tablets and popped them into his mouth, swallowing the pills dry. He'd gotten good at that.

Maybe he should buy stock in the company, he mused. Ryan screwed the cap back on and threw the bottle into the drawer.

He wondered if this mess with the body washing ashore had contributed to his headaches in any way. God knew it hadn't helped.

People were whispering all the time now, looking at him oddly as he passed. As if he were somehow responsible for this latest ripple that was upsetting life as they all knew it in Red Rock.

Why would he kill someone he didn't even know?

Being at the top had its rewards; he would be the first to admit that. But it certainly had its shortcomings, too. Maybe it was the work of these headaches, but lately, it seemed to him that while everyone looked up to you, they wanted to see you taken down. If not all the way, then at least several pegs.

As if by having you come down, they could somehow rise up themselves.

Ryan closed his eyes and frowned. The dark thought was foreign to him. He didn't normally dwell in these nether regions.

It had to be the headaches. They were making him think like this. Like someone he didn't know.

He couldn't help wondering if, as the townspeople and police officers believed, he was related somehow to that poor, unfortunate man who'd met his end somewhere around here.

What if it was another one of Cameron's seed? God knew his late brother had enjoyed dallying with as many women as he had time for.

Ryan opened his eyes again and sighed. The headache was still pounding, making him nauseated with its intensity. He supposed he was going to have to bite the bullet and go to see the doctor, but God, he hated to be poked and prodded.

Worse than that, he'd always been a firm believer that no news was good news, at least as far as health was concerned. What if the news was bad? What if these headaches were indicative of something that time, patience and the best medical care that money could buy wouldn't erase?

What if there was no way to cure the cause of the problem?

Ryan ran his hand along his forehead again, impatience taking hold. Damn it, this wasn't like him. That kind of attitude would have never allowed him to come as far as he had.

To be the man that he was.

The man, he reminded himself, that his Lily loved. Ryan focused on his blessings. He had a good family and finally had the woman his heart had always belonged to.

What more could a man wish for?

Besides a way to get rid of these damn headaches, he thought sarcastically.

There was a soft knock on the door. So soft that he was tempted to ignore it. But his secretary wasn't the kind to intrude on his time unless it was absolutely necessary.

"Come in." He didn't raise his voice, afraid that would exacerbate his headache.

The door opened. His secretary looked both annoyed and distressed. The annoyance intensified as she glanced over her shoulder, while keeping the door firmly ajar so that only her face was visible to her employer.

"I am sorry to bother you, Mr. Fortune, but there are two people from the Red Rock Police Department to see you. Do you want me to send them away?" She sounded almost eager for his permission.

Ryan smiled, appreciating the woman's fierce loyalty. Other people might whisper, but the core of supportive staff, family and friends he kept around himself didn't. And when he came right down to it, that was all that was really important—the people he cared about.

He beckoned her forward. "No, that's all right. Show them in."

His decision met with his secretary's obvious disapproval, even though she inclined her head. "Very well, Mr. Fortune."

The next moment, she opened the door all the way and stood back, admitting Officer Gabe Thunderhawk and Detective Andrea Matthews.

Andrea approached him first, nodding a greeting, as formal as she had been the last time they'd met, in the coroner's office.

"You're a hard man to get hold of, Mr. Fortune," she said, sitting down in the seat Ryan indicated.

Gabe followed suit, although in Ryan's judgment, the man looked as if he would be more comfortable standing.

"I'm a very busy man, Detective," Ryan replied.

Andrea was pleased that Ryan Fortune didn't minimize her rank, the way some other people she'd dealt with had. Still, this might just be the man's way of falsely putting her at her ease so that she was liable to miss something.

Wasn't going to happen, she thought. If Ryan Fortune

was somehow involved in the death of the unidentified man who had washed up on shore, then his position in the community notwithstanding, she was going to nail him for it.

She had too much to prove not to.

It took everything for Ryan to carry on a regular conversation and not wince from the pain. The headache stubbornly refused to abate. His own voice seemed to echo in his head, scraping against the inside of his skull.

Maybe he just needed a prescription for a stronger headache tablet, he told himself. Something for migraines.

The thought heartened him slightly.

"We've been able to digitally enhance that birthmark on our victim," Andrea informed him.

Ryan barely nodded. Vanessa had called him about her own visit from the police. She'd been furious for him, bless her. It had taken him a while to calm her down. "So I've heard."

Andrea leaned forward. "Then you must have also heard that, from what we can see, it appears to be identical to yours."

"I'm having that looked into." He didn't like the idea of an unknown connection between himself and the dead man any more than the police apparently did. Except that he knew he was innocent.

"Maybe you could share that information when you get it," Gabe suggested politely, before Andrea could say anything. It earned him an annoyed look from the detective.

"Count on it." Opening the drawer, Ryan took out the aspirin bottle again and downed two more pills.

Andrea looked at the bottle he was holding. "Something bothering you, Mr. Fortune?"

"Just a nasty headache." He shut the bottle back in the

drawer and rose to his feet. "I have a board meeting to get to, so if there are no further questions…" He left his sentence hanging as he walked to the door and opened it.

Andrea stood up and crossed the room, albeit none too happily. "We'll be in touch," she said as she passed him.

He inclined his head ever so slightly. "I'm sure you will. Goodbye, Detective. Officer."

He closed the door firmly behind them and took a deep breath. He had exactly twenty minutes to pull himself together before the board meeting. With any luck, the headache should be abating by then.

He could only hope.

Eight

"But why can't I come?"

Luke trailed after his mother, his arms wrapped around the bottom of the tent she was bringing in from the garage. His lower lip was stuck out in a pout as he unceremoniously dropped his end of the tent on the living room floor.

Savannah carefully parked the tent out of the way beside the sofa. Taking a breath, she looked down at her son.

"Because you're going to have more fun with Aunt Vanessa. She and Uncle Devin are going to take you to the amusement park and to the movies, and knowing Aunt Vanessa, I'd guess she's probably going to let you stay up as late as you like instead of hustling you off to bed the way that your father and I do." Savannah had thrown in mention of Cruz because she wanted Luke to think of them as a united front. In truth, Cruz hadn't been home for the boy's bedtime in a while now, ever since the pace had picked up on the ranch.

The information made Luke break out in a big smile, immediately erasing the pout from his lips.

"Okay, I'll go," he announced.

"I thought you might change your mind." Savannah leaned over and ruffled his hair.

Looking around, she surveyed the living room. It was filled with all kinds of camping supplies. She'd been depositing gear in the living room in preparation for the weekend ever since Cruz had okayed the idea. She wanted to be sure they had everything they were going to need to make the two days and nights as comfortable as possible.

Unlike some people who went camping, Cruz didn't believe in taking a camper out into the wilderness. To him, that was cheating. He liked doing it the way his ancestors had, with a bedroll spread out beneath the stars. It was all Savannah could do to convince him that a sleeping bag would be better than a blanket tossed on the hard ground.

The tent, she knew, was going to require a little finessing on her part. But taking it along was important to her. She was just going to have to convince him about it.

She heard the back door open and then close. Cruz, she thought with a smile. Even though this was officially the beginning of their weekend, he'd wanted to personally feed the new horses and clean them, including the one he was going to be keeping, Diablo.

He did it for bonding purposes, and she knew it was important to him, so she'd said nothing when he'd walked out early this morning. Anticipating this, she'd told Vanessa not to come for Luke until after nine.

She heard the water running in the kitchen. Cruz had stopped for a drink. "Savannah?" he called.

"In the living room," she answered, then braced herself.

He didn't disappoint her.

"What's that?" he asked as soon as he walked into the room. Cruz moved the end of the tent with his boot and looked at her quizzically.

The item was new. She'd deliberately gone into Red Rock for it yesterday and had the clerk load it on the truck for her. She and Luke had taken it out of the box before she'd carried it into the garage and hidden it behind the aluminum ladder Cruz used when he painted the house.

She pushed her hands into the front pockets of her jeans and rocked back on her heels. "It's a tent."

He raised his eyes to hers. "I can see that. What's it doing here?"

"Lying on the floor," Luke answered, then covered his mouth as he stifled a giggle. "Mama and me dragged it in from the garage."

"Mama and I," Savannah corrected, the teacher in her unable to leave the sentence alone.

Cruz was still eyeing her, waiting for a real explanation. "Whose is it?"

She took a deep breath. "Ours."

He sighed, hooking his thumbs on the loops of his jeans, looking down at the tightly wrapped tan object as if it were a trussed-up deadly snake he was trying to figure out what to do with. He had never owned a tent, never made use of one. And he had no intentions of starting now.

"Savannah, you know how I feel about sleeping in a tent. You might as well be sleeping in a camper—or back home in your own bedroom."

"Not quite," she countered. She thought he carried his convictions a little to the extreme. She glanced at their son, who seemed to be all ears, listening to every word. What she had to say didn't need any witnesses, especially not a pint-size one. "Luke, why don't you go up to your room and make sure you've got everything for your stay at Aunt Vanessa's?"

"'Kay." Like a tornado, Luke dashed out of the room and ran up the stairs. She heard the sound of his small boots overhead as he reached his bedroom seconds later.

Even with him out of earshot, Savannah still lowered her voice. She nodded at the tent. "We don't have to sleep in it."

Cruz's dark eyebrows knitted together. "Then why bring it?"

Did she have to spell it out for him? "Because we can use it when we…you know."

For a second, Cruz didn't know. And then he looked at her, amused. Married five years and she could still blush. "Make love, you mean?"

"Yes." She cleared her throat. "I thought we could use it for…privacy."

His amusement grew. "Who's going to see us? The owls?"

She lifted her shoulders and let them fall again. "You never know." There might be other campers in the area, or hikers. She didn't want to take any chances. Savannah decided to turn the focus back on him. "I thought you were such a private man."

"Yes, I am. About the stuff that goes on between us, not about…this." His eyes skimmed over her form and he laughed. He came up behind her as she sorted out a few things to be put in their backpacks. Cruz could feel himself getting in the mood even though they had yet to load a single thing onto the truck. He put his hands on her shoulders. "What you're talking about is as natural as the stars themselves." He turned her around to face him. "A warm campfire, a beautiful woman. A man who's way overdue," he admitted with a sexy grin as he verbally painted the scenario for her. "As natural as the stars above," he repeated.

Savannah sighed. Maybe she'd become a little too prudish these days. After all, the first time they had made love was in the stable on Ryan Fortune's property. There'd been a party going on at the house, and any number of people could have walked in on them.

She hadn't cared then. And she wanted to get back to a time like that. Desperately.

Cruz kissed the side of her neck, making wonderful things happen inside of her. Anticipation went up another notch.

If he kept this up, she thought, they wouldn't need to go anywhere. She was going to attack him right here where they stood.

"The tent stays home," she agreed with a deep sigh.

"That's my girl." He laughed and put his arms around her, drawing her closer to him. He took comfort in the way they easily fit together. "You know, I'm glad you came up with this idea."

Her eyes sparkled as she said, "Yeah, me, too."

Reading the look in his eyes, she inclined her head. But the kiss that was to come was aborted by the sound of pounding footsteps overhead.

As he came flying down the stairs, Luke's feet resonated as if he were at least twice as heavy as he was. He made it from his bedroom to the living room in less than ten seconds.

"Aunt 'Nessa's here!" he announced at the top of his

lungs. He came to a skidding halt when he saw his parents together. His face contorted. "Ugh, yucky stuff." There was no missing the condemnation before he dashed to the front door.

With a touch of reluctance, Savannah disentangled herself from Cruz. "He should be very grateful for 'yucky stuff.' If it wasn't for that, that little man wouldn't be here."

Hurrying from the living room, Savannah made it to the front door a beat after Luke. The boy had already pulled it open.

Savannah did her best to look reproving, if not angry. "What did I tell you about opening the door when you hear someone knocking?" she chided.

"But it's Aunt 'Nessa," he protested. "I saw her from the window in my room. You said that about strangers. Aunt 'Nessa's not a stranger."

"Got you there," Cruz called out.

"Some support you are," Savannah said over her shoulder.

Walking into the house, Vanessa grinned. She ruffled the boy's hair with affection. "So you were watching for me, handsome?"

Luke laughed, his dark eyes dancing. "I was looking for my stuff. Mama wanted me to make sure I didn't leave anything behind."

"Can't have that," Vanessa agreed. And then she leaned toward him and confided, "Wouldn't want you to get bored."

Coming forward, Cruz brushed a swift kiss on Vanessa's cheek by way of greeting. "You know what you're letting yourself in for?" The question was voiced only half in jest.

"Fun," she answered without hesitation.

"Fun, huh?" Cruz looked dubiously at Savannah. "You said she was here when Luke jumped through the coffee table?"

Savannah nodded. "She was here."

He laughed and shook his head as he turned back to Vanessa. "You've got nerves of steel, woman," he told her.

"I'm a Fortune," she answered. Though it was an amiable conversation, there was no missing the pride in her voice. "We're bred to put up with everything."

"Speaking of which," Savannah interjected, switching gears, "how is your father handling all this body business?"

Luke's waning interest was suddenly piqued. "There's a body?" he asked, his eyes as big as proverbial saucers. "What body? Whose body?" His head moved back and forth from one adult to the next so fast, his straight dark hair swung about his head like a silky black curtain swaying in the wind.

"We're raising him to be an investigative reporter," Savannah quipped as she looked at her friend.

"I can see why." Vanessa laughed.

"No body," Cruz told Luke firmly, using a tone that Luke was familiar with. It brooked no nonsense, no trivial queries.

Luke shoved his small hands into his back pockets, looking dejected.

Vanessa had a feeling that Cruz was attempting to spare her. She knew this wouldn't be the end of the boy's questions. Those would go on until he had answers he was satisfied with.

"Just some stranger who was in Lake Mondo," Vanessa told him.

Clearly she was the one with the answers, so Luke aligned himself with her. "Who is he?" he pressed.

Vanessa raised her shoulders in an exaggerated shrug. "He didn't say."

Luke frowned, cocking his head just the way his mother did when she was pondering something, Vanessa thought. "Can't you make him talk?"

"No." Although amused at his tenacity, she was beginning to realize that in placating the boy, she'd launched herself onto a slippery slope. What would it take to get him to abandon the subject?

"Betcha you could," Luke countered suddenly, a sunny smile lighting up his small face. "You could make anyone say anything."

Vanessa looked at Savannah over the boy's head. "I think I've just been flirted with." She laughed again.

"It's the fatal Perez male charm," Savannah told her, glancing over her shoulder at her husband. "It starts young."

"You forget, I grew up with Cruz." Vanessa winked at her friend, indicating that the remark was just as harmless as it seemed. Not for the world would she have Savannah thinking that there had ever been anything beyond friendship between her and the man her father had once employed as a horse whisperer. "I've already been forewarned." And then, dismissing the subject, she glanced toward the spot where the coffee table had been. A small folding card table stood there now. "I see you got rid of the evidence."

Cruz had carted it out of the house the next day. "My brother-in-law says he can make us a new one," he told her.

"That's good." She saw the look on Savannah's face.

Her friend was anxious to get started. Not that she blamed her. Vanessa glanced down at Luke. "Well, what do you say we get going, handsome?"

Rather than take the hand she extended to him, Luke grabbed the suitcase his mother had helped him pack last night. With his other arm, he clutched several of his toys. One slipped out and he tried again, this time with more success.

"Okay!" he called out.

Vanessa laughed at the comical figure he made as Savannah went to help her son make a more graceful exit.

Just then there was a loud knock on the front door. It wasn't a polite tapping, but one that demanded immediate attention.

And then, as if unable to wait, the person on the other side turned the knob and swung the door open.

It was Jaime, the youngest of the hands and the most recently hired. His eyes had a frantic look as they scanned the room, searching for Cruz. The second he saw him, he blurted out, "Boss, we got trouble."

Savannah immediately stiffened. Every syllable the young ranch hand uttered pounded a stake farther into her heart.

"What's wrong?" she asked, before Cruz had a chance to say anything.

The young man's head bobbed up and down in a delayed but polite acknowledgment of both her and Vanessa. Belatedly, he stripped his sweat-stained hat from his head as an added sign of respect.

The words tumbled from his lips like white-water rapids in the river. "We dunno how it happened—"

"How what happened?" Cruz demanded. If he didn't make the man begin at the beginning, who knew how long it would take to untangle what he was saying?

"Hank's a good rider," Jaime babbled, as if defending the other man.

Cruz saw fear and confusion mounting in Jaime's blue eyes. He grabbed the younger man by the shoulders, as if the very action could help him focus.

"What happened?" Cruz repeated sternly.

With great effort, Jaime pulled himself together. Now the words flew from his mouth like bullets. "His horse spooked," he cried. "Hank fell off—except that his foot was stuck in the stirrup. His horse ran and Hank was dragged. We got to him as fast as we could—"

Cruz heard Savannah stifle a cry behind him. "How bad is it?" he asked.

"We think he broke his arm. Billy's with him now. We need the truck to take him to the hospital in town in case something else is broken we don't know about."

Cruz nodded grimly. "I'll be right there." But as he began to head toward the door, he realized that Savannah was right behind him. He stopped and turned around. "What are you doing?"

She looked at him, surprised that he would even ask. Hank wasn't just someone who worked for them, he was a friend. "I'm coming with you."

He frowned. The ranch was clearly his domain, and the hired hands were his to take care of. "There's no need, Savannah."

Was he trying to keep her out of this? How could he? What happened on the ranch was both their responsibility, not just his. "If Hank's arm really is broken, I can immobilize it well enough to get him to the hospital." She saw the skepticism in Cruz's eyes. Her stubborn streak rose to the foreground. "I had the first-aid course. You didn't."

He lowered his voice, although it could still be overheard by Vanessa. "You're pregnant, Savannah," he pointed out.

"What is *that* supposed to mean?" Of all the stupid, tunnel-vision thing to say... Savannah struggled to curb her annoyance at the comment as best she could. "I won't be bandaging him with my uterus, Cruz." She pushed past him to the front door. "The kit's in the truck. I packed it last night," she explained.

Cruz relented, knowing he was just being overprotective. But he didn't like her being exposed to things like that.

"Think of everything, don't you?"

The hint of admiration in his voice went a long way to placating her indignation.

"No," she told him, "I don't." She certainly hadn't thought that, halfway out the door, this would happen to impede their getaway plans. She glanced over her shoulder toward Vanessa. "Um—"

Vanessa put her hands on Luke's shoulders, drawing him to her. "Don't say another word. Just go. Luke and I will be waiting for you when you get back."

Luke looked up at her. "We can't go to your house?"

She exchanged knowing looks with Savannah. "Not yet, honey. Let's see how Hank is first."

Savannah hurried out the door, praying that Jaime was an alarmist and that things were really better than he thought they were.

They weren't.

Hank's arm turned out to be broken, just as Jaime had told them. Savannah used two rods she found in the back of the truck to help immobilize the tall ranch hand's arm.

She'd picked up the rods the other day, intending to use them to stabilize saplings she wanted to plant in the front yard. She hadn't had time to get around to the planting; now she was glad she hadn't.

"Ever think of being a nurse?" Hank asked her as he watched her encase his arm and the rods with the wide bandage.

"I'm a mother, which means I'm already part nurse," she told him. Luke and his mishaps had been the reason behind her taking the first-aid course.

Finished, Savannah cut off the last of the bandage and knotted it before looking at Cruz. "We're ready to roll."

"I can still drop you off at the house," Cruz offered as he climbed back behind the wheel to take Hank to the hospital. He was leaving Jaime and Billy behind to round up the horses and bring them back to the corral.

She remained in the back with Hank, who was lying down on the blanket she'd spread out for him. Miraculously, other than scrapes and bruises, the cowboy appeared to have sustained no other damage to his six-foot-four lanky frame.

"That would take you out of your way." The house was back in the other direction, away from Red Rock. "Just head for the hospital," she told him.

Parking in the emergency room lot, Cruz jumped out of the truck. "Stay here," he ordered Savannah as he went through the doors.

He was back in a couple of minutes with an orderly and a wheelchair.

Savannah smiled at Hank as she got out of their way. "Looks like you're going to ride in in style."

Hank grimaced getting off the truck. "I'd rather be on the back of a horse."

Savannah laughed. "Seems to me that's what got you into this in the first place."

Hank gave her a sheepish grin as Cruz and the orderly helped him into the chair.

The waiting was the worst of it. Cruz spent the better part of the hour and a half they were forced to wait pacing.

"It's not going to be any faster if you wear a hole in the floor," Savannah told him.

"I can't sit still."

"I noticed."

Finally, the doctor came out to find them. The expression on the young resident's face was optimistic as he approached them.

"It's a clean break," he told them. "There's every indication that it should heal in a couple of months."

"A couple of months," Cruz echoed. That meant that Hank would be of little use to him on the range and only of minimal use in the stables. All this while collecting pay.

It felt as if he just couldn't catch a break, Cruz thought ruefully, then realized the irony of the thought.

Dr. Neubert caught the inflection in Cruz's voice and interpreted it correctly.

"Could have been a lot worse," he said, looking from the ranch owner to his wife. "I would like to keep Hank here overnight, just to watch him and make sure there's no concussion. He did take a nasty fall and bring dragged didn't help. But he's young, resilient. That all acts in his favor. He should be good as new once he heals."

"Yeah." Cruz pressed his lips together, feeling overwhelmed. "Once he heals."

Because he seemed to have slipped into his own world, Savannah took the lead. "Thank you, Doctor," she said, shaking the young physician's hand.

"That's what I'm here for," Dr. Neubert responded.

The next moment he was being summoned to another room, and he hurried down the hall, leaving Cruz and Savannah alone.

Cruz leaned against the wall, staring off into space, making calculations. He carried a small health policy for both himself and his men with a major insurance company. To be affordable and keep costs down, the policies all came with sizable deductibles. One he felt it was his duty to cover, since the accident had happened on his land, during the execution of Hank's normal duties.

More payments he hadn't counted on, Cruz thought darkly.

Not only that, but now, for all intents and purposes, he was another man short, at least until Hank learned how to manage to get work done using only one arm.

But that wasn't the least of his problems. Looking toward Savannah, Cruz braced himself.

She wasn't going to like what he had to say.

Nine

The tension inside the truck was thick enough to touch. Cruz said nothing, not wanting to spend the trip home arguing with his wife.

Savannah read the signs correctly and tried to fill the time with small talk. She hoped that if she could remain upbeat, she wouldn't hear what she was afraid of hearing. That their trip was being postponed. Indefinitely.

"He looked pretty good." They'd both gone to see Hank after his surgery. The ranch hand had been cleaned up, but seemed very uncomfortable, though that had more to do with the hospital gown he was forced to wear than the battering he'd sustained.

"For a man who'd been dragged by his horse, yeah, he looked pretty good," Cruz allowed.

"It could have been a lot worse, just like the doctor said," she pointed out.

There were times when her cheerfulness was like a haven for him, but this was not one of them. Sometimes it could be damn annoying, like a pebble inside his boot.

"Yeah." But he didn't see how it could have been. Not when he was forced to take up the slack, and he had next to no time in which to do it.

They were pulling up in front of the house. Savannah saw that Vanessa's car was still parked beside the garage. Her friend hadn't changed her mind and taken Luke home with her.

It didn't feel like a good sign, Savannah thought.

She slanted a glance toward Cruz. It was time to broach the subject. She began slowly. "I guess you could ask Billy or Jaime to go pick up Hank from the hospital tomorrow."

Single, with no family in the immediate area, Hank Jeffers lived in the mobile home they kept on the property along with Jaime. Only Billy went home at night to his wife and daughter. He lived close enough to La Esperanza that it didn't present a hardship to him or interfere with his work.

"I could," Cruz said as he turned off the ignition and pulled up the brake.

She'd been with him long enough to finish at least some of his sentences. Mostly the ones, it seemed, that she didn't like.

Savannah turned toward him in the cab. "But you won't."

Cruz stared straight ahead through the windshield, not really seeing the house. "No, I won't."

Damn it. Savannah clenched her hands in her lap. She'd known this was coming. "The only way you can pick him up is if we don't go on the camping trip."

He shrugged carelessly, his expression unreadable. "Half the day is gone already."

"Which means that half the day is still ahead of us," she pointed out stubbornly. Why did he always have to be so damn negative?

He spared her a glance, annoyed. Why was she making this so hard for him? "Savannah, weren't you listening in the hospital? We're a man short—when we can't afford to be."

Yes, she thought, she'd been listening. And what she'd heard—and hoped she hadn't—was the somber sounds of a death knell. The death of something she'd held dear to her heart and had been trying desperately to breathe new life into.

But you can't breathe life into something that was dead, she reminded herself.

"And it's going to make that huge a difference if you're gone from the ranch for—" she glanced at her watch "—thirty-six hours? That's all I'm asking for, Cruz. Just thirty-six hours." Wasn't she worth that amount of time? That amount of effort? Why was she always last on his to-do list?

Cruz got out of the truck, slamming the door a little harder than he'd intended. He was struggling to hold on to his temper. He felt like a man dangerously on the edge of falling over. Under ideal conditions, he wouldn't even be having this discussion. There would be men enough to cover for Hank until he was better.

But the conditions weren't ideal. Maybe someday, but not yet. Why was that so damn hard for Savannah to comprehend?

Rounding the hood, he went to open the door for her, but she'd already gotten out.

"You're asking for a hell of a lot more than that," he told her.

She didn't like his tone. "What?" she heard herself demanding, her patience stretched to the limit. "What am I asking for, Cruz? Your manhood? Your pride?"

"Stop talking like a teacher for once," he snapped. "This isn't about philosophy, this is the real world. And in the real world, I have a ranch to run and I'm already one man short," he reminded her. "Losing Hank temporarily makes things that much worse. I can't just waltz off now because I feel like it. There's too much to take care of."

He caught hold of his temper, knowing that none of this was Savannah's fault. He was frustrated about the turn of events and he was taking it out on her.

"Look," he began again, "I don't want to yell at you, but you're not helping the matter any by pushing my buttons."

"Buttons?" Savannah stared at him incredulously. He made her sound as if she was trying to pick a fight over some trivial thing instead of trying to make him understand what was happening to them. "Now who's talking philosophy? I'm not pushing buttons, Cruz, I'm trying to save our marriage."

At her words, he waved an impatient hand. "Stop exaggerating."

She wanted to shout at him that she wasn't exaggerating, that they were in a crisis situation and he was just too blind to see or acknowledge it. But she knew that shouting, that making him feel as if he was at fault, wasn't going to solve anything. It would only escalate matters.

Desperate, she tried to take another approach in order to resolve the problem. "Look, you were going to hire another hand anyway—"

"Exactly my point," Cruz interjected. "We're already shorthanded."

And whose fault was that? she wanted to demand. Money was tight, but if the hired hand lived on the property, then that was part of his pay and they could manage to take on one more. Besides, more work would be done and they could handle more horses. But Cruz had dragged his feet. Because he'd been a hired hand himself and seen the world from that end, the standards he had for one were higher than most. It made hiring difficult.

"So hire one already," she pressed. "Stop being so damn fussy and just take someone." From where she stood, she could make out the corral. Billy and Jaime were busy grooming the horses that Cruz was preparing to sell by the end of the month. In her opinion, the two had turned out to be better than average, but it was hard getting that admission from Cruz. Had he always been this hard-nosed? Had love made her miss that in the beginning? "If they don't work out, then you let them go. You've done it before."

She was missing the obvious, Cruz thought. "That doesn't help the weekend."

She waved a hand at the men in the corral. "Billy and Jaime will manage. It's not like they're a pair of city slickers who just stumbled onto our property without a clue."

Cruz stuck to his guns. "The only way they managed before was because Hank was there to watch them."

She had him, she thought. Her mouth curved in triumph. "I thought Hank wasn't good enough to be a foreman."

"Stop twisting things."

"I'm not the one twisting things," she argued. "You keep changing your story to suit the occasion." Because he looked as if he didn't know what she was talking about,

Savannah reviewed the recent events for him. "When I told you that you should consider making Hank your fore-man, you said he didn't have what it took yet. But now you're saying he was what kept Billy and Jaime working right." Her eyes narrowed in a silent challenge, daring Cruz to get out of this. "You can't have it both ways. Which is it?"

He threw up his hands. "I don't have time to argue."

As he began to leave, she shifted so that she was in front of him again, impeding his escape. "Apparently you do, because that's what you're doing."

Cruz's dark eyes widened as he looked over her shoulder. Savannah turned around to see that Vanessa and Luke had come out of the house.

"Hi, you two. How's Hank?" Vanessa called from the front porch. Luke came out behind her and ran toward his parents.

Savannah recovered first, pulling herself together and masking the inner turmoil she was feeling. Shielding her eyes from the sun so she could see Vanessa and Luke bet-ter, she answered, "He's got a broken arm."

Luke's mouth dropped open. "But he'll be all right?"

Savannah smiled. However many wrong turns her life had taken, at least she had Luke. The best thing that had ever happened to her.

A bittersweet pang wove through her as she looked at him. "Yes, honey, Hank's going to be all right. He just needs a little time to mend."

"You know," Vanessa said, taking the three steps down from the porch, her eyes on Cruz, "if you need any tem-porary help, I'm sure my father could send over a couple of men from the Double Crown to tide you over—"

Because it was Vanessa and he knew she meant well, Cruz wasn't curt with her. But he didn't appreciate the thought that he needed any kind of charity. Even, indirectly, hers.

"Thanks for the offer, but I don't need any help." His tone was crisp, dismissive.

Savannah's eyes widened. How could he ignore an offer like that? "But you just said—"

His eyes were steely as he turned them on her. "I can take care of it."

He absolutely refused to be viewed as the poor Mexican the rich Fortunes had to bail out. His pride wouldn't allow him to accept charity, no matter what form it came in, or how well-intended the person offering it was. Accepting charity put you in someone's debt, and he was determined to be in debt to no one.

Vanessa crossed to Cruz. "Wouldn't be a problem," she insisted. "I know for a fact that things are a little slow on the ranch right now. Spring branding's over and I'm sure—"

Cruz's lips moved into an obligatory smile that lasted all of ten seconds. "I said thanks, but no thanks," he repeated. "We can manage."

Savannah drew in a ragged breath. She was tired of being the dutiful wife, tired of waiting for Cruz to come to his senses. She'd spelled it all out for him and still he refused to understand, refused to meet her even a quarter of the way.

She was his helper, his bookkeeper, the mother of his children, and she got less consideration than the newborn colt he'd mothered last month.

It had to change.

"No," she said firmly, her voice low and threatening to break as she looked at him. "We can't manage."

Cruz firmly believed that husbands and wives did not contradict each other in front of people, even old friends. He looked at her sharply, his eyes narrowing. "Savannah…"

It was a warning.

Vanessa offered Savannah a quick, apologetic smile. "Maybe I'd better go," she said quietly. But as she started to move, Luke placed himself in front of her, preventing her from going to her car.

"I'm not going with you?" Disappointment echoed in his voice.

Vanessa stroked his cheek. "No, honey. I don't think your parents will be going away. Maybe some other time," she promised.

"No," Savannah said suddenly, surprising both Vanessa and Cruz with the intensity of her voice, "his parents are going away. At least one of them is."

About to walk off to the corral, Cruz stopped and spun on his heel. He was so stunned by her words that he forgot there was anyone else within hearing. "What are you saying?" he asked evenly.

She pulled her courage to her. Giving in and waiting for him to come to his senses wasn't the way to go. It clearly wasn't working.

"I'm saying that maybe Luke isn't the only one who's going to Vanessa's." She looked at her friend. "Got room for one more?"

Vanessa slanted a glance toward Cruz's angry face before asking Savannah, "You?"

It was too late to back down, and maybe that was a good thing. "Me."

"Yes, Savannah," Vanessa finally replied, "but maybe you should think this over."

Savannah knew that if she hesitated, she was done for. Her knees already felt weak. But her spine was firm, and she was resolved. No guts, no glory.

And maybe, a small voice inside her whispered, *no husband.*

She raised her chin, determined. "I have thought this over." Her words were in reply to Vanessa, but it was Cruz she looked at as she said, "Maybe we need some time apart." And then she did turn to Vanessa, a silent entreaty in her eyes. "Could you go upstairs with Luke and pack a few more things for him?"

Savannah was aware that her friend would recognize the excuse to get the boy away. Knew, too, that Vanessa cared enough about Luke to protect him from seeing his parents fight, which no doubt was coming.

Without a protest, Vanessa took Luke's hand in hers and squeezed it. "C'mon, handsome, let's see what else we can find to take with us."

Maybe it was Savannah's imagination, but her son seemed reluctant as he followed Vanessa back up the porch steps to the front door. Just before he crossed the threshold, he looked over his shoulder at both of them, his small face worried.

It was as if he knew that something awful could be happening here.

"Okay," he agreed. His eyes went from his mother to his father. "But don't yell, okay?"

It almost broke her heart. This more than anything convinced her that she and Cruz needed to clear the air between them, before it started to take its toll on their son.

"We won't yell," Savannah promised, forcing a smile to her lips for Luke's benefit. It was gone the second that he was.

Cruz waited for the front door to close before he turned on Savannah. "You're not being reasonable."

She should have known he was going to say something like that.

"I'm being more than reasonable," she countered. "I've been reasonable for five years now. Reasonable as I've watched you work more and more, not less. Reasonable as I've waited for you to put us first, not last."

"That's ridiculous." He struggled not to raise his voice. "You and Luke aren't last. Damn it, Savannah, it's not a contest—"

"Certainly feels like one."

He went on as if she hadn't said anything. "—and five years isn't enough time to establish a ranch."

Didn't he get the point? He was investing all this time he wouldn't be able to use again. "But it's five years that you won't get back. Five years out of your son's life that you missed. And five years out of ours."

She was beginning to make his head ache. "What are you talking about?" Cruz demanded. "You and Luke are here every day."

"And you've taken that for granted," Savannah retorted.

He could see the ranch hands looking in their direction. Damn Savannah for picking here and now to have this out with him.

"Oh, don't start that stereotypical garbage with me. I don't take you for granted. I depend on you."

She wasn't going to allow him to wiggle his way out of this with words. Yes, he depended on her, but in a careless, offhanded manner. She wanted some sign of appreciation, some hold on his time. "Even the ranch hands get a bonus."

He stared at her as if she'd begun babbling in a foreign

tongue. "I hand over all the money to you. What more do you want? For heaven's sake, you're the bookkeeper."

"I don't want money, I want you," Savannah reiterated for what she felt had to be the umpteenth time.

"And how the hell is your going to Vanessa's supposed to accomplish that?"

She wasn't thinking beyond the moment. All she knew was that she needed to get away. Being around him, being neglected by him, just hurt too much.

"I don't know. Maybe it'll make you miss me. Or maybe you'll find out that you're happier without me." She squared her shoulders, a soldier about to face the front lines for the first time. "Either way, it's about time we knew."

His eyes searched her face, still not believing what he was hearing. "Then you're serious?"

She pressed her lips together to keep them from trembling and giving her away. "Never more."

He was having trouble letting the concept sink in. There had to be something he was missing. Savannah couldn't be saying what he thought she was saying. "You'd leave me."

It sounded so cruel when he said it. But she couldn't waver, she told herself. If she did, she was lost. She had to be strong. For both their sakes. "I think we need a breather to sort things out."

His eyes narrowed. "You leave this house, our marriage is over."

It was the wrong thing for him to say.

Savannah wasn't about to allow herself to be threatened or backed into a corner.

In her opinion, she'd tried harder than any three women to make their marriage work. Over the last year, she'd made all sorts of excuses for his behavior, for his absences, but that was all in the past. She was tired of bending over backward, tired of pretending everything was going to work out when it just kept getting worse.

It had taken her a long time to come to grips with this, but she couldn't live like this anymore, stressed out with nothing positive to focus on.

Maybe she'd never had what she'd wanted, and had just been deluding herself all along.

As she'd told Cruz, it was time for her to find out.

Savannah straightened her shoulders, her eyes on his. "Well, then, I guess it's over, because I am going to Vanessa's house."

Cruz glared at her, furious. He would never have believed she was capable of this, of giving him an ultimatum, forcing him to go against everything he believed in just because she needed to be reassured that he cared about her.

Cared about her? Hell, everything he'd done from the moment he'd first realized she was carrying his child five years ago had been for her. This ranch was for her and Luke and the baby who was coming.

Children needed to be proud of their father. And she was asking him to sacrifice everything because she was feeling insecure.

Damn it, he loved her, but he wasn't going to be ruled by her. What kind of a man would he be if he allowed that to happen? What kind of an example would he be setting for his son?

"I guess it is," he told her tonelessly.

There was no door to slam in his wake. There didn't have to be. His receding footsteps echoed in her brain long after she'd hurried into the house.

To pack.

Ten

Vanessa was standing at the top of the stairs, watching for her when Savannah walked into the ranch house. "How is everything?"

Savannah looked up at her. "It's been better."

It was hard getting the words out over the huge lump that had suddenly materialized in her throat. Savannah refused to cry in front of her friend, afraid that once she began, she wouldn't be able to stop.

Her hormones still felt as if they were in high gear. And right now there was an ocean behind her eyes just waiting to be unleashed.

She pressed her lips together, determined to work her way through this crying jag that threatened to overtake her. She looked up at Vanessa. She knew she'd made an assumption earlier, but that had been just for Cruz's benefit. She'd secretly hoped that if he thought she was walking out on him, it would suddenly force him to realize that he needed to reassess his priorities, to put his family first the way he once had.

Swallowing, she cleared her throat. "Can I stay with you?"

The moment she asked, Vanessa flew down the stairs. Luke was in his room, still sorting through his toys to find his five favorite ones the way she'd asked him to. The two friends were alone together. She went to Savannah and threw her arms around her.

"That goes without saying, you know that. You and Luke are welcome to stay with us for as long as you want." And then she drew her back to study Savannah's face. "Not that it won't be wonderful having my best friend within reach again, but are you sure you want to do this? We both know that men can be very pigheaded where their pride is concerned."

A sad smile curved Savannah's mouth. She willed her tears back. "Yes, I know. But this is my last stand, Vanessa. If I can't get Cruz to realize that he misses me, if I can't get him to come around and see what it is he's throwing away because he's taking it for granted, well, maybe I've been fooling myself all along." She glanced at the portrait over the fireplace. It was of the two of them, done shortly after Luke had been born. "Maybe I've been in love with a man who really doesn't exist anymore." Squaring her shoulders, she looked back at Vanessa. "If that's the case, I might as well find out now and move on with my life."

Move on.

It sounded so modern, Savannah thought. As if she really could extract Cruz from her heart and push forward. There was never going to be anyone else in her life but him. If she lived to be a hundred, she knew she was never going to love another man. Never give another man her heart the way she had Cruz.

Damn him.

Vanessa had her doubts about the wisdom of what Savannah was proposing to do, but she knew that her friend felt as if she had to do something. And who knew, maybe this would shake Cruz up.

Still, she thought there might be another way to get things back to the way they were. "Have you thought about going to a marriage counselor?"

Savannah laughed shortly, shaking her head. "That would require time, which is exactly what Cruz and I are arguing about now. Time and sharing," she added ruefully. "Cruz isn't about to admit to himself that we have any problems, let alone talk to anyone else about them. And a stranger?" She hooted. That was just never going to happen.

"A professional," Vanessa pointed out, although, knowing Cruz, she had to admit that Savannah was right. The man would never go for it. When it came to his own, he was as private as a clam.

"A professional stranger, that's how Cruz would see it." The smile faded from Savannah's lips. "No, this is the only way."

Vanessa hesitated, then posed the question that was hovering between them like a fearsome specter. "And if he doesn't come around? What if he decides to wait you out instead?"

That possibility had already occurred to her. "Then I'll take the next step." Savannah steeled herself as she uttered the word. "Divorce." Even so, it made her physically ill just to say it.

Just to think it.

It took very little for Vanessa to feel her friend's pain. She knew how she would feel, having some judge and a pile of legal papers declare her union to Devin over. "Oh, Savannah."

For Vanessa's sake, Savannah forced a smile to her lips. It was hardly more than a hint of one.

"We're not there yet. Come help me pack," she urged. "I'm feeling a little scattered right now. I could wind up packing the hangers and leaving the clothes."

"You could start a whole new look." The smile Vanessa offered her friend was soft, encouraging. "Who knows, on you it might work." She slipped her arm around Savannah's shoulders as they went up the stairs.

He watched them go.

Cruz was in the second corral, the one farther from the house, where he trained the horses he was getting ready to sell. To take his mind off the argument he'd just had with Savannah, he was grooming Flaming Arrow, the chestnut quarter horse he'd bonded to first.

As he drew the curry comb through the mare's mane, he saw Savannah come out of the house with Luke. She had a single suitcase with her, as did the boy.

For a second, something akin to hope shot through Cruz.

And then he saw Vanessa carrying two more suitcases. Putting them into the cherry-red Mustang, she doubled back for more.

His heart turned to lead within his chest.

It was really happening, he thought. Savannah was leaving him, along with their son.

His hand tightened so hard around the curry comb it seemed in danger of snapping in half.

Savannah put Luke into the back seat, then rounded the hood and got in behind the wheel. The car door closed and she started up the vehicle. The sound of the engine transcended everything else, all the noises around him.

The bucket of soapy water he'd used to wash the mare stood at his feet. Cruz never brought his anger to the corral, to the horses. He knew them to be sensitive creatures, capable of knowing when there was discord around them. He wanted to bring out the positive aspects of their personalities in order to turn them into good working animals.

But right now his anger rose up like bile in his mouth.

Unable to stifle it, he kicked the bucket next to him. The soapy water sloshed over the sides before the pail fell over. The suds sank into the dirt, leaving behind a residue of foam.

"Something wrong, Boss?" Billy called out.

Cruz made no answer, but went back to brushing the mare.

Billy, always cheerful to a fault, walked over and picked up the pail and the sponge that had fallen out of it. At twenty-three, the young cowboy had finally stopped growing, topping off at six foot three inches. He wore his curly blond hair longer than was the style. On humid days, it swirled around his head like a sunny crown.

The ranch hand glanced toward the house and saw two cars leaving.

"Thought you and the missus were going on a camping trip."

"Well, we're not," Cruz stated. Then he shrugged carelessly. "Hank's accident changed that."

Billy wiped his damp hands on the back of his jeans. "Oh."

His knowing tone had Cruz looking sharply at the younger man.

Billy's easygoing grin only widened. "Ever tell you my philosophy about women, Boss?"

"No." The single word was meant to be a warning that he didn't want to hear whatever Billy had to say.

The nuance was wasted on the young man.

"They're like roses," he told Cruz. "The prettiest ones have the worst thorns and need a lot of—what d'you call it—finesse." He grinned at being able to find the right word. "That way you can handle them without losing blood." The grin widened again. "But they're always worth it."

Jaime came up to join them. He clamped a hand on Billy's shoulder. "This from a guy who's only been with one woman his whole life," he hooted.

"Or so I've said," Billy answered, with a smug wink that was meant to make the two men wonder.

Jaime went back to what he was doing. Only then did Billy look at Cruz. His expression had turned sober.

"You ever need to talk, Boss," he told him, lowering his voice so that Jaime wouldn't overhear, "I'm here."

There was no point in taking the kid's head off, Cruz thought. He had no idea what was really going on, and he meant well.

Cruz nodded toward the stables. "Well, while you're here, Billy, see what you can do about getting the colts fed."

The cowboy inclined his golden head, glad to be of use. "Right away. And then maybe you'll let me watch you work with the cutting horses."

"Maybe," Cruz echoed.

It seemed enough for Billy.

* * *

The fund-raiser for children with HIV was held in the largest ballroom of the poshest hotel in San Antonio. From one end to the other, the huge room was filled with beautiful people. At first, it had left Melissa "Wilkes" in awe.

She'd seen celebrities rubbing elbows with billionaires, self-made as well as second and third generation. Toying with her third glass of wine, a vintage one from someone's private collection, Melissa had trouble deciding which group was her favorite.

The richest, she supposed, because money created its own aura of celebrity. The thought made her smile as she took another sip.

The wine wasn't going to her head, it was empowering her. Clarifying her vision of things to come.

Things she was going to make happen.

Hooking up with Jason and posing as his wife had been one of the smartest things she'd ever done, she decided.

And now she was focused on doing something even smarter.

Cutting Ryan Fortune out of the herd of desirable men and making him her own.

Granted, the man was currently married, but Lily Fortune was his third wife. A man who'd married three times wouldn't be averse to marrying a fourth, Melissa mused knowingly. And she certainly had no problem with not being the first.

As long as she was the last.

Melissa Fortune.

It had a nice ring to it.

And it would come with a nice ring, she thought, feeling slightly giddy. The one on Lily Fortune's left hand could easily be used to guide fog-enshrouded ships lost at sea back to the safety of the harbor. Melissa already knew that she was going to ask for a bigger one when it was her turn.

That it wouldn't be her turn never crossed her mind. Confidence was the hallmark of her personality. Young, gorgeous and well-endowed, Melissa always got what she set her cap on.

And now she was determined, very determined, to better her lot.

When Jason had come into her life with his scheme to discredit Ryan Fortune because of some "injustice" he'd said the man's ancestors had visited upon his grandfather, she had agreed to pretend to be his wife. It was to give him the air of respectability he needed. She'd done it on a lark. At the time she'd felt that anything was better than withering on the vine the way she'd been.

But now that she'd had a taste of the good life, like the Fisherman's Wife, she wanted more.

And more came in the guise of Ryan Fortune.

Jason had rubbed off on her, she mused, looking around at the people mingling in the ballroom. She intended to do him one better.

Because Jason knew how to orchestrate things in his favor, he had managed to be the right man in the right place when they were looking to fill a position in Fortune TX, Ltd., the company headed by Ryan's nephew, Logan. Jason knew that there was trouble within the company and that Ryan was coming in as an adviser. He'd made sure to get noticed, quickly making a name for himself.

So much so that he wound up catching Ryan's attention. The man had a reputation of rewarding those who worked hard on his behalf.

The thought amused her. Little did Ryan realize that what Jason was working hard at was his eventual discredit and demise.

Which had been all one and the same to her until she'd decided otherwise. Until the good life had opened its doors to her and shown her all the possibilities that being married to someone rich and powerful could really provide.

Jason was never going to be that person. There was something ultimately destructive about him. He was fixated on Ryan's ruin.

She was fixated on her own elevation.

Working behind the scenes, Melissa had laid her own groundwork for the future. She'd made sure to join all the charities Ryan gave his time to. She'd arranged things so they were in places at the same time. She made it so that every time he turned around, she'd be there. Helping.

And every opportunity she had to flirt with Ryan, to flatter him, she grabbed. When Jason took her to task about it, she'd said that she was only doing it to divert the old man's attention from Jason's true purpose. And Jason, the fool, had bought it.

Up to a point.

But she didn't care what Jason thought or didn't think. Her goal was quite plainly the seduction and winning of Ryan Fortune.

It certainly wouldn't be as odious as some of the things she'd done. At age fifty-nine, Ryan Fortune was still a very attractive man with a full head of dark brown hair and a solid, muscular build from years of working on a ranch.

But even if the man looked like Rumplestiltskin, she wouldn't have cared. He came with enough money to make him extremely desirable to her.

Finishing her wine, Melissa put the fluted glass down on a nearby table and picked up another from a passing waiter. She drank deeply, feeling the liquid course through her veins. Feeling as if she could conquer the world.

Or at least one dapper man.

She intended to go about her plan from two different directions. The first was to appeal to Ryan, which she assured herself she already did. That he hadn't taken her up on her less than veiled suggestions of meeting with her in one of the hotel's suites didn't deter her. He'd succumb by and by.

The second part of her plan was to create discord between Ryan and his wife. She couldn't very well offer the man a shoulder to cry on if there was nothing to cry about, now, could she?

So she would give Ryan something to complain about. His wife's unfounded jealousy.

A smile played on Melissa's lips as she contemplated the scenario. She could be very, very understanding if need be. And the price was right.

Patience was never her long suit, but she managed to bide her time.

And then she saw her chance to begin sowing the seeds of discord and suspicion. A vision in soft lavender, Lily excused herself from Ryan's side and went to the ladies' room.

Melissa lost no time in following her. She knew that Jason was somewhere on the floor, undoubtedly networking and setting down the foundation of his own trap. It was time she went about laying down hers.

The ladies' room was located in the center of another long

hallway, the path marked by a patterned wallpaper that pleased her eye only because she knew it to be so expensive.

As she made her way after Lily, Melissa had the feeling she should be marking her trail with bread crumbs. The soft lighting in the hall did little to help her get her bearings.

The actual ladies' room and outer salon were larger and far more spotless than the shack she'd grown up in. Strolling in, Melissa did a quick survey of the stalls, taking inventory.

None of them appeared to be in use. Melissa relaxed a trifle. This would go more smoothly now.

Bathed in the tinted blue lights coming from the ceiling, Lily Cassidy Fortune was standing before one of the aquamarine sinks, carefully freshening her makeup. Fifty-nine herself, she was still very much a handsome woman.

Ryan Fortune obviously had an eye for beautiful women, Melissa thought. Which was a mark in her favor, because she was younger than Lily and was certain she was more attractive.

Putting her purse down on the counter beside Lily's, Melissa nodded at the woman. Lily smiled in return, that vague sort of smile exchanged between people attending functions such as these.

"Hello, Lily."

The tone of familiarity was impossible to miss. Lily's eyes narrowed slightly as she looked at the younger woman. "Do I know you?"

"Not yet." Melissa paused, her tone pregnant. She really enjoyed saying the next part. "But your husband does."

Another perfunctory, fleeting smile graced Lily's lips. She was trying not to be dismissive, but knew her Ryan was a very, very busy man. She counted herself lucky that she saw him as often as she did and that he tried to make sure they had dinner together every night. Sometimes it was served as late as eleven, but the hour didn't matter, as long as they spent time together.

"Ryan knows so many people, it's hard for me to keep track," Lily replied lightly.

"For the record, I'm Jason Wilkes's wife, Melissa." The last name was fake, as was her marital status. To be honest, Melissa had no idea what Jason's real name was, but knowing it didn't figure into her plans. She was out for herself, not Jason.

Lily's face lit up at the mention of the man's name. "Oh, yes, Ryan speaks very highly of Jason." Her eyes shifted in the mirror to look at the other woman. "You should be very proud."

"So should you." Before Lily had a chance to murmur the obligatory thank-you, Melissa continued, malicious triumph in every word. "That is quite a stud you have. You know, at his age, most men are already relegated to the sidelines, operating at diminished capacity if they're operating at all, if you catch my meaning. But not Ryan." She smiled. "He's right there, leading the charge."

Lily's hand dropped to her side. Leaving her comb on the counter, she turned to look at the younger woman. She found her intimate tone offensive. Granted, the words were vague enough to give a business interpretation—if not for the word *stud*.

That brought what the woman said into a whole different light.

Lily's eyes took on a haughty appearance. "Excuse me?"

She'd gotten to her, Melissa thought. That had been easy.

"Am I embarrassing you, Lily?" She feigned kindness. "You know, that might be your problem. If you want to hold on to a man like Ryan, you can't be so easily embarrassed. As a matter of fact—" she leaned closer, noting how the woman stiffened in response "—you have to be willing to try all sorts of new and different thing sexually. Otherwise, he might get bored and start to stray." And then she smiled smugly. "But I guess my saying that is like talking about closing the barn door after the stallion's left it." She deliberately selected a suggestive metaphor.

Lily firmly believed in her husband's fidelity. Not because she could account for his every moment, but because she trusted him.

"What are you implying?" she asked.

The smile Melissa allowed to unfurl across her lips was slow and sensual. It was done for effect, to make Ryan's wife uneasy. In truth, Ryan had never done anything more than shake her hand, but there was no reason for his wife to know that. It didn't serve Melissa's purposes to have Lily believe her husband was faithful or innocent.

"I would think that would be obvious to even a…" Melissa paused, as if searching her memory banks. "What was the term Ryan used? Ice Princess, yes, that was it."

Lily gripped the side of the counter. "Are you saying that you and Ryan…?"

The smile on Melissa's face was pure malice. "What do you think?"

Anger colored Lily's cheeks. Ryan was a good man, a decent man. He wasn't the kind who sneaked around behind his wife's back. There was no need for that. Granted, he'd been a little secretive lately, but she'd just assumed it was work related. He often had a lot on his mind. And now, with those awful rumors about that dead body circulating around town, it was no wonder he'd become pensive and quiet.

Lily drew herself up. "I don't believe you."

Melissa appeared unfazed. "That, dear lady, is your prerogative." She picked up her purse, never even going through the ruse of putting on makeup. Her mission, for now, was accomplished. "They say that wives are the last to know." She moved toward the door. "Usually because they're so wrapped up in their own little worlds, they don't see that they've lost their husband's interest."

"Ryan loves me," Lily declared.

Melissa merely nodded, a look of pity entering her eyes. "You go right on believing that, Lily. Who knows? You might even win out." She paused for effect, then said, "But I doubt it."

And with that, she walked out again.

A laugh of satisfaction bubbled up in her throat as she heard what she assumed was Lily's evening bag hitting the ladies' room door with a thud.

Score one for the home team, Melissa congratulated herself.

Eleven

"Just what the hell do you think you were doing?"

His fury getting the better of him, Jason Jamison fired the question at the woman posing as his wife the moment they were inside his car. With the windows raised, he didn't even wait until they had pulled away from the hotel.

The little bitch could ruin everything.

Melissa smoothed out her gown beneath the seat belt. She hated the way seat belts always made her dresses wrinkle. "I'm sure I don't know what you're talking about."

Jason raced the sports car through a light as it changed to red. "Don't you? You were trying to get closer to Ryan Fortune than his underwear."

He'd witnessed it early in the evening. Melissa standing close to Ryan, taking his arm, all but pressing her ample chest against it.

It was all Jason could do to keep up appearances during the course of the evening. Like a butterfly unable to find somewhere else to land, Melissa kept returning to Ryan. At one point, drawing closer, Jason had managed to overhear her side of the conversation. It was as he suspected. She was all but throwing herself at the man.

This wasn't what he'd had in mind when he'd sworn to avenge his late grandfather, a man who had been forced to live out the end of his days in squalor because of the Fortunes.

When Melissa laughed in response to his observation now, the sound annoyed the hell out of him. The rage Jason had been keeping bottled up inside of him, the rage that had led him to murder already once in his life, threatened now to rise over the top and spill out on this woman who appeared to be turning on him.

His hands tightened on the steering wheel. He envisioned her neck in its place.

"Why, darling," she cooed in the same sultry voice she'd used on Ryan, "I'm just trying to help."

Right, like he really believed that, Jason thought. He had eyes. Did she think he was born yesterday?

"The only person you're trying to help is yourself," he said.

Her eyes narrowed as she looked his way. The interior of the car was dark and masked the contempt she knew was in them.

"Must be the company I've been keeping." The car shot through another light. To her right, a car came to a screeching halt to avoid a collision. She stiffened, then took a deep breath to regain control. "Hey, careful, you don't want to get us killed before your triumph, do you?"

The malevolent smile softened as she turned toward him. "Really, Jason, you need to get control over that temper of yours or it'll undo all that nice work you've put in at Fortune TX, Ltd., making a name for yourself. Ryan won't want to play with you anymore if he thinks you're a hothead."

Jason hated the belittling tone she was taking. Hated the sound of her voice. If it wasn't for him, she'd still be living in that small town, hustling for dollars instead of living the high life.

"You let me worry about Ryan Fortune," he growled. And then, because his ego demanded it, he couldn't help boasting, "I've got him eating out of my hand."

Melissa moved the car's sun visor so that she could see herself in the passenger vanity mirror. Fussing with her hair until she was satisfied, she turned up the visor again.

"Try to think of me as added insurance. That's why you brought me into this thing, isn't it?"

"I brought you into this because having a wife made me look more respectable. Fortune seems to think that a married man's more stable than a bachelor." This time, he couldn't make the light even if he gunned his engine. With effort, he put his foot on the brake. The car fishtailed before it came to a stop. He turned to glare at her. "But if he thinks my wife is a two-bit whore…"

If he meant to insult her, he was going to have to do better than that, Melissa thought, amused at his paltry attempt. Unlike him, she didn't have a low flash point. It took a great deal to make her lose her temper and take her eyes off the prize. In this case, the prize was Ryan Fortune. Or rather, *his* fortune.

The idea of being one of the richest women in Texas held great appeal for her.

"Not two-bit," Melissa corrected indulgently. "Never two-bit." She sighed, leaning back in the passenger seat.

"I won't bother arguing the whore part. There's no point. We both know that's true." She lightly feathered her fingers through his hair and traced the outline of his ear. "Otherwise I wouldn't be here with you now, would I, sugar?"

He jerked his head back, still very much annoyed rather than aroused. "Stop that."

Dropping her hand, Melissa shifted and sighed dramatically. "Whatever you say." And then, because it suited her to irritate him, she added, "I'm sure that Ryan Fortune wouldn't tell me to stop that. He looks like a man who could definitely use a little wild time in the sack." Her mouth curved as she thought about the older man. She bet he could still show a lady a good time if he put his mind to it. The kind of man who believed in slow loving instead of wham-bam-not-so-much-as-a-thank-you-ma'am, which represented Jason's style. "That wife of his looks like she's got a stick up her butt."

Obsessed with his mission the way he was, Jason could smell trouble. "Don't you ruin this for me," he warned, his tone dangerous. "I've put in a lot of time, planning his humiliation and death."

Melissa closed her eyes, tired of Jason's voice. Tired of having to settle for what he had to offer when there was so much more she could have.

"Yes, I know. You've told me. Over and over again, you've told me. I don't think anyone likes the sound of your voice better than you, Jase." And then she gave him her attention one final time before withdrawing into silence. "You might try learning something from him before you kill him, lover. Right now he's twice the man you'll ever be."

It was like waving the proverbial red flag in front of a charging bull, and she knew it. Jason didn't disappoint her.

"What the hell is that supposed to mean?" he demanded hotly.

She refused to give him the satisfaction of cringing. As crazy as he was, Jason didn't scare her any. If she wanted to, she could make him jump through hoops, she told herself. After all, she'd gotten him to bring her along, hadn't she?

Hitched her star to a freaking sociopath, she had, but it suited her purposes at the time. She would cut him loose the moment she had Ryan Fortune.

"Just something for you to chew on, lover." With that, Melissa leaned back against her seat, closed her eyes and shut Jason out entirely.

The house was too empty.

When Cruz returned to it at night, it stood right there waiting for him.

The loneliness.

It stood waiting in a shell of a house that was lost in darkness.

Just like his soul, Cruz thought, shutting the door behind him and flipping on a light.

Rather than illuminate, the light seemed to intensify the darkness outside its reach.

For a few days, it had almost been tolerable. He'd gone to pick up Hank the day after Savannah had left, and put the ranch hand up in the spare bedroom. Hank had remained two days, then pronounced himself fit to go back to work and back to the trailer.

Not that he blamed him, Cruz thought. The loneliness had probably gotten to him, too.

Cruz walked into the kitchen and went to the refrigerator out of habit rather than need. He had to keep up his energy.

The refrigerator was only half-full. Savannah had purposely not shopped the day before she'd left because they were supposed to be going away.

Supposed to be.

The words hung in the air before him, haunting him.

With a grunt, he cleared his head, then took out a hunk of cheddar cheese Savannah had used for grating, and threw it on the table.

Dinner.

Cutting a few pieces, he forced down a slice, then took a glass of water and all but drained it. Toying with a second piece, he pared it down to little more than pea-sized. Then he gave up.

There was no point in going through the motions. He just wasn't hungry.

Not for food, anyway. What he was hungry for was the sound of Savannah's voice. Hungry for a thud resounding from somewhere in the house that told him Luke was at it again.

Repackaging the cheese, Cruz put it back in the fridge and pulled out a beer instead. He popped the top and took a long, healthy swig.

Who would have ever thought it? he jeered to himself. Somewhere along the line, when he wasn't looking, Romeo had been replaced by a dyed-in-the-wool family man. The so-called stud who had prowled the Double Crown Ranch, hooking up with any woman he wanted, sometimes more than one in a single night, had turned into his own father.

The realization made Cruz shiver.

He would have never believed it, had anyone told him this would come to pass even as little as six years ago. But there was no denying that was what he'd become. A family man.

And right now his family was missing.

Taking his beer with him, Cruz wandered over to the bay window in the living room and looked out. A full moon cast a mournful light over the land. His land.

There was no stirring inside of him when he thought that. That was Savannah's doing.

Truth was, she had ruined him. Ruined him for any other woman. All he could think about was her, night and day.

But damn it, if she thought he was going to come crawling to her and apologize even though he was in the right, she was sadly mistaken. He could wait her out. After all, he was in their house. She was the one who was living on someone else's good graces. Eventually, she had to come home, right? She wasn't going to deprive Luke of his father just because of her pride.

Cruz drained his beer and crushed the can in his hand. He didn't want her coming back because of Luke, he wanted her coming back because of him. Because she felt as damn awful as he did.

He stared at the reflection of the lonely looking man in the bay window. Who the hell was he kidding? He wanted her to come back no matter what.

Just as long as she was home, that was all that counted.

With a sigh, he went back to the kitchen to throw the can away.

He still took his cell phone with him whenever he left the house in the morning. Just in case she called.

But with each day that went by, he was less and less certain that she was going to call. And more and more certain that he hated this life without her.

Nine days she'd been gone. Nine whole days and there hadn't been so much as a peep out of her. Damn stubborn woman, that was what she was.

He opened the refrigerator again to get another beer, then changed his mind and slammed the door. The sound echoed throughout the house, mocking him.

Feeling as if he were going to crawl out of his skin, he crossed back to the front door. Just before he went out, he felt for the cell phone in his front shirt pocket. Taking it out, he checked the battery to make sure it wasn't ready to die on him the way it had the first day. But there was enough of a charge. He tucked it back into his pocket and left the house.

He headed back to the stables.

Inside, he went to the stall where Diablo was kept, separated from the other horses like some kind of visiting dignitary—or a prisoner assigned to solitary confinement. It was done for a reason. Cruz didn't want the horse's attitude infecting the others, and he wanted the animal to feel isolated, except from him.

But tonight he was the one who felt isolated and in need of company.

Diablo's eyes were on him the moment he approached the stall. Maybe even the moment he entered the stable, Cruz mused.

Smiling, he picked up a curry brush just before he walked into the stall. "So how's it going?" he asked the horse.

The black stallion continued to eye him much the way enemies who had called a truce did. The trust was evolving, but it was a slow procedure.

Nothing good was ever hurried, Cruz thought. Except that first night when he'd made love with Savannah. Then it had been all flash and fire, passion and needs. And it had been good.

Damn it, he wanted her. Wanted her now. In his arms, in his bed. He wasn't sure just how much longer he was going to be able to hold out.

The animal was still watching him. If he concentrated, Cruz could almost feel the stallion's thoughts forming.

He'd come out here to force Savannah from his mind. Being around horses had always been soothing to him. It was as if this was where he was meant to be. Where he belonged. But now that his life had been upended, he felt as if he belonged nowhere.

"I've let you have your lead," he said to Diablo in a soft, soothing voice, "but you know this can't go on forever. You're the horse, I'm the master. It's just something you're going to have to get used to." With each word he uttered, Cruz moved closer. In the beginning, Diablo would barely tolerate him in the same corral. This was the horse's home ground and yet the animal didn't rear, didn't posture as Cruz approached. They'd made progress.

Too bad he couldn't make the same kind of progress on his own home ground, Cruz thought.

"But that doesn't mean you're any less a magnificent creature, just because you let me train you," he continued. "See what I'm saying here? It's a two-way street. You get yourself a skill and you get yourself rewarded." Cruz felt that the animal was listening to every word. Others scoffed that horses didn't understand people, but he maintained it was people who didn't understand horses. "A fine cutting horse like you will bring in a pretty penny. You'll be regarded as something special."

Drawing closer to the animal, Cruz put out his hand. The horse didn't move. Cruz slowly began to stroke the animal's muzzle.

It had taken him nearly two weeks to get to this point. Slow and steady, his mind whispered. The end was worth waiting for.

Then, to his surprise, the horse inclined his head and seemed to nuzzle him. Cruz laughed, feeling pleasure, something that had eluded him for quite some time now.

Especially these last nine days.

"Funny, I'm so good with horses and so bad with females. Well, female," he amended, picking up the brush he'd brought into the stall and beginning to slowly draw it along the length of the horse's back. "One," he told Diablo. "The only one I want."

Diablo looked over his shoulder at him.

"Okay," Cruz allowed, "I'll brush harder, talk less."

He only kept half his word. He brushed harder, but he kept on talking. And as he talked, he began to feel better.

Savannah had no idea what to do with herself.

She was accustomed to working hard all day long, and now was very much at loose ends.

And at the mercy of the rampaging emotions inside her.

There was no house to take care of, no husband to look after, no books to balance. Her days weren't even filled with Luke anymore, because there was always someone to play with him or take him places. Vanessa and Devin certainly enjoyed spending time with the boy, and now that news of what she'd done had reached Cruz's family, his sisters and parents all came by to make sure that Luke didn't feel neglected.

The boy was having the time of his life.

She wished she was.

"You're supposed to be using this time to recharge," Vanessa would tell her whenever she asked for something to do.

"I'm overcharged," Savannah had complained the last time. "A battery is supposed to be put to use, otherwise the charge just leaks slowly away."

Tonight when she'd voiced her restlessness, after the housekeeper had cleared away the dinner dishes from a table where only the two of them sat, Vanessa reminded her, "You're a guest here."

"I'm a vegetable here," Savannah countered.

No matter where she went in the house, she couldn't find a place for herself. And hospitality had nothing to do with it. She wanted Cruz back in her life, but not on the old terms.

The trouble was, she was afraid he wouldn't subscribe to any new ones.

After dinner, Vanessa had led her into the entertainment room to watch a movie. The moment it was over, Savannah couldn't remember what it was about. She had no interest in watching movies. No interest in watching anything while life as she knew it drained away.

"I never thought that I'd say this," she sighed, "but I don't think I can stand having any more free time."

Vanessa aimed the remote at the DVD player, causing the disk to eject. "We could go out. I could take you shopping," she suggested, getting up. "It's late, but there are still some stores open in the mall." She tried to warm Savannah to the idea. "You could get some new clothes—my treat."

She didn't even bother to say she could buy her own clothes. She knew Vanessa only meant it as a gesture of friendship. Instead, she pointed out the obvious. "I have no one to wear them for."

Vanessa pretended to sniff. "I think I've just been insulted."

"You know what I mean."

Her friend walked over to the six-foot-tall maple carousel filled with DVDs on all four sides. Taking the ejected disk out, she replaced it in its jacket and then returned the movie to its place.

"Yes, I know what you mean." Turning from the shelves, she looked at Savannah. As soft-spoken as her friend was, Vanessa knew how stubborn she could be. "Have you tried calling Cruz?"

A dozen times her hand had gone to the telephone receiver. A dozen times she'd pulled it back. This was the hardest stand she'd ever taken, even harder than the time she had kept her baby's parentage a secret to keep Cruz from feeling as if he was honor bound to do the right thing and ask her to marry him.

"He hasn't tried calling me," she pointed out.

Stubborn. No other word for it, Vanessa thought with a shake of her head.

"This isn't a game of chicken, Savannah, where you wait until the last minute before you do the sensible thing."

"No, it's not," she agreed. "It's not a game at all." If it had been a mere game, she would have called it off a long time ago. But this was different. Her future hung in the balance. "He doesn't even miss me enough to phone."

Vanessa gave her a pointed look. "Cruz could say the same thing."

She hadn't expected that sort of a reply from her friend. "Whose side are you on?"

Vanessa put her arm around Savannah's shoulders. "The side of truth, justice and the American way." And then, turning Savannah to face her, she added more soberly, "What I'm in the middle of is two very stubborn people trying to see who holds out the longest. You know he loves you."

That was no longer a given as far as Savannah was concerned. It hadn't been for a while now. "Do I?"

Even as she asked, Savannah's hand went over her belly. She could feel a small swelling there now. By this time, most women were larger. Even so, she'd detected the baby's movements.

She still wasn't feeling right. She often felt sick, not just in the morning, but all day long. It was as if her body was somehow completely out of sync.

Vanessa saw her expression and misread it. "C'mon, Savannah, you know he does."

"Then why isn't he here?"

"Because he's Cruz. Because his male pride won't let him make the first move."

If he loved her, he would, Savannah thought stubbornly. "There're some things more important than pride."

Vanessa laughed. Savannah was preaching to the choir. "Words right out of my mouth."

Savannah stopped. Did Vanessa think *she* was holding out because of pride?

"I'm not doing this out of some misbegotten sense of pride, Vanessa. I'm doing this to see if I mean anything to him anymore. I've stood in last or next to last place for a long time now, listening to him tell me that this is all for me, and for Luke. Lip service," she insisted. "That's what it is. Just lip service. Cruz Perez wants to be the big, respectable horse rancher, not me." She felt like crying again and it was all she could do to hold herself together. "All I want is Cruz."

Vanessa ached for her, but there was nothing she could do to change what was. "Well, this is part of him," she said, referring to the man's need to make a name for himself.

Savannah prowled around the room, her footsteps echoing on the highly polished maple floor. "It never used to be."

Vanessa moved in front of her. "Oh yes, it was. Ever since I could remember. This was always part of who and what he was. He wanted to make something of himself, to be someone. And loving you made him go after his dream."

"So now it's my fault he's spending most of his waking hours away from home?" She sighed. "A gesture, Vanessa, all I want is a gesture. Something to make me feel that I'm not just part of the furniture to him."

Vanessa looked at her friend's stomach, a smile curling her lips. "You're pregnant. I doubt if he would have made love to the furniture."

Savannah laughed, shaking her head. "You are not helping."

"But I made you smile. My work here is done." She stepped out of the room, walking to the den.

The doorbell chimed in the background. Vanessa glanced at her watch. It was almost nine. She wasn't expecting anyone. Devin was out of town on an assignment the FBI had sent him on until late tomorrow afternoon, and Luke was spending the night with his grandparents.

"Can you get that for me, Savannah?" she called. "See, don't ever say I won't let you do anything around here."

Though she'd just sat down on the sofa, Savannah pulled herself to her feet. Her body, as trim as ever, felt oddly heavy.

Walking over to the door, she glanced at the security camera. Her heart stopped, but she told herself it was just wishful thinking. Her imagination was running away with her, nothing more. The glass sometimes distorted the image.

She yanked open the door and saw that the image hadn't been distorted.

Cruz was standing on the doorstep, his hat in his hand.

Twelve

He couldn't remember when he'd felt this awkward. Feeling like that had never been part of who and what he was. Yet standing here like a supplicant before the woman who'd been his wife for over five years, the one person in the world he'd have thought he'd never feel uncomfortable around, he felt awkward.

Cruz ran the rim of his hat nervously through his fingers, hating the feeling that was vibrating inside of him.

Wishing he were somewhere else.

Knowing he couldn't have been anywhere else than here. Because, even if his father hadn't unexpectedly shown up on his doorstep earlier this evening to "talk some sense into your fool head," Cruz knew he would have found himself here tonight. A man could go only so long without the air he breathed, and whether he admitted it to himself or not, Savannah had turned out to be like the very air to him. Vital for his survival.

She looked tired, he thought. And wan. Did she miss him? Had she spent the last ten nights thinking about him the way he had about her?

He didn't know if he wanted to know the answer to that.

Cruz nodded toward the inside of the house. "Can I come in?"

Savannah had never seen him like this. Subdued. As if someone had siphoned the very spirit out of him. The Cruz she knew could have been the poster child for pride, and at times, for arrogance, because he believed in himself and felt that others didn't.

But this was something different, something new. Had she done this to him? Or was there another reason he looked like this now? Was there something wrong at the ranch? Something he felt she had a right to know?

She stepped back and opened the door farther, admitting him by her action as well as her words. "Of course. Please, come in."

"Who is it, Savannah?" Vanessa called out from within the depths of the house.

"It's Cruz."

Savannah only realized that she'd all but whispered his name when Vanessa called out again, repeating her question. "Who?"

Clearing her throat, trying not to lose herself in the small, seductive smile that came to her husband's lips, Savannah raised her voice. "It's Cruz."

"Cruz?" Delight followed on the heels of surprise as Vanessa popped out into the hallway and peered toward them.

"So it is. Cruz," she repeated, openly marveling at the

miracle of his appearance. She nodded at him. "Well, time for me to get scarce. I'll see you in the morning, Savannah." Vanessa looked significantly at Cruz. "Unless of course…"

Her voice trailed off, leaving Savannah to put her own ending to the sentence.

"Right," Savannah murmured, still staring at her husband, taking nothing for granted until she had it spelled out for her.

God, he looked better than she remembered. But weary around the edges. Was that her fault? She was afraid to credit herself with having too much of an influence in his life. That way, if he wasn't here because he missed her, but for some other reason, she wouldn't hurt too much.

Or at least not any more than she was already hurting.

Unaware of her surroundings, her attention completely riveted on Cruz, Savannah wasn't even sure if Vanessa immediately disappeared or took her leave slowly.

"How's Luke?" he finally asked in an attempt to keep himself from telling her how much he'd missed her. How empty everything seemed without her presence. At home, even if he didn't see her, just knowing she was somewhere around had made all the difference in the world to him. He was only just now realizing that and wondering what had happened to the man he'd been.

Savannah finally closed the door behind him. "Luke's fine. He's with your parents tonight."

"I know." He turned around to look at her. "I mean, my father told me."

Was that why he was here? Because Ruben had told him to make amends? Her father-in-law had always been nothing but sweet to her, as if he understood the stubbornness she had to put up with.

"He called you?" she asked.

Cruz laughed softly. His father had walked in on him as he was nursing a beer for dinner. He'd taken the can right out of his hand and retired it to the table. Hard. Then he'd gone on to state what an idiot Cruz was and how he would have never believed it of him, even during the worst of times.

"He came over. To lecture." A rueful smile played on Cruz's lips. "My father hasn't tried to lecture me since I was fourteen years old." Looking at her, he debated the next admission, then decided to be honest. "He seems to think I'm screwing up."

She tried to picture that and failed. Savannah shook her head. "Somehow I can't see that word coming out of your father's mouth."

"Words to that effect," he allowed. Crossing to the living room, he changed the subject. "So Luke doesn't ask after me?"

"All the time." Because she needed something to do, she straightened the magazines on the coffee table, putting all three into a neat pile. "But he thinks he and I are taking a vacation here and you couldn't come because you're too busy."

Cruz tossed his hat onto the sofa, an indication to her that he was going to stay. At least a little while. "How did he come up with that?"

"I told him. I thought it was easier than telling Luke that Mama and Daddy are taking a vacation from each other."

He took a step toward her, unable to tolerate any sort of distance between them. "Is that what this is? A vacation?"

She shrugged, hating the way they were tiptoeing around each other, and wanting to throw herself into his arms and have him tell her he loved her at least half as much as she loved him.

"Words to that effect," she said, echoing his previous statement.

He blew out a breath and shook his head. "Well, if that's what this is, it's the worst damn vacation I've ever been on."

Hope scrambled up inside of her. "Oh?"

The machismo that had kept him from coming here the very first night she'd left floundered and then vanished. Somehow, saving his pride didn't matter anymore. Having her back in his life, in his bed, did.

Reaching out, he touched a strand of her hair. The feel of it almost undid him. "The house is empty without you." His eyes met Savannah's. "Everything's empty without you."

Another woman, maybe even Vanessa, Savannah thought, would have stood back, would have waited until more was said. Another woman might have savored her triumph or silently demanded more.

But another woman didn't ache the way she did, didn't feel as if half of her was missing the way she had these last ten days she'd spent without him.

Unable to restrain herself any longer, she did what she'd wanted to do from the moment she'd opened the door to see Cruz standing on the doorstep. She flung herself into his arms.

The surprise that drenched him melted away instantly, to be replaced with an entire whirlwind of emotions he'd had no idea were dancing through him until this very moment.

Cruz closed his arms around her and pulled Savannah to him. He sealed his mouth to hers as he cupped the back of her head and tilted it toward him.

The moment he kissed her, the dam broke. All the emotions came pouring out.

Like a starving man being unexpectedly offered a slice of bread, he couldn't hold himself back.

Cruz kissed her over and over again. Her mouth, her eyes, her nose, and then her mouth again. The hunger didn't abate; it grew in depth and volume.

"Damn it, Savannah, but I've missed you."

The words echoed in her head like the sound of church bells on Christmas morning. Had he given her a diamond necklace, she wouldn't have been as thrilled as she was at this very second.

Her body heated instantly to his touch, to his presence. Her arms were around his neck and she cleaved to him, pressing her body against his. Desires that she'd been unable to bury all this time rose to the surface, demanding recognition.

Demanding release.

They both knew they couldn't pull apart. Both knew that the degree of chemistry traveling between them wouldn't be satisfied with merely heated embraces and a few feverish kisses.

He didn't want to stop kissing her, stop holding her. But he couldn't give in to what his wife had awakened within him right here.

When he picked her up in his arms, she gave no sign of resistance. Savannah curled her body into his, silently telling him she wanted him as much as he wanted her.

His voice thick with desire, with unspent emotion, he asked, "Where are you staying?"

"The bedroom off the den," she breathed. When he lifted an eyebrow in mild confusion, she laughed. He looked so like Luke just then, this man she loved. "I'll guide you," she promised.

The bedroom wasn't far. But in the time it took to reach it, the anticipation within her had more than doubled.

By the time Cruz crossed the threshold and closed the door behind them, she was ready to tear the clothes from his body with her bare hands.

Who would ever have thought that she could feel like this? That lovemaking would matter so much to her? Growing up, she had never seen her parents so much as touch each other with affection in passing, or bother saying a kind word. She'd believed that all marriages disintegrated, and she never wanted to be in that position, sharing a space with someone she would rather not.

It had taken falling in love with Cruz to show her the well of emotions she'd left utterly untapped, the emotions she hadn't known existed.

Her life had begun in Cruz's arms.

And now it was resuming.

Releasing her after setting her on her feet again, Cruz cupped her face between his hands and kissed her lips lightly, as if it was a step he'd forgotten and was now trying to rectify.

But though he meant to be gentle, to go slowly, having been without her all this time had caused something to happen. It had made him feel almost insatiable.

The gentle kiss grew like a flower that had been fed some sort of magic ingredient, causing it to triple in size in a very short amount of time.

Quickly, he hurried Savannah out of her clothes, while she did the same with him.

She knew that she should have held out at least a little longer. Since Cruz wanted her so much, it would have been a good time to negotiate terms, to have him agree to working less and going away with not just her, but with Luke, for a longer vacation.

But she was incapable of negotiating, incapable of hooking up one thought with another. All she could think of was that he was here, that he had stepped off the high pedestal of his principles and come to her.

And that she missed him more than she'd thought was humanly possible.

Their clothes in a heap on the floor, they delighted in tangling themselves up in each other's bodies.

Blood thundered through Cruz's veins as he kissed her, stroked her, reacquainted himself with every inch of her. It felt as if a lifetime had gone by instead of ten days. He knew it had been longer than that since they'd made love.

Feeling the sharp sting of deprivation, he strove to make up for lost time. And in doing so, he felt as if he had returned home after a long, soul-punishing absence.

Until the moment he touched her, the moment he kissed her, he hadn't fully appreciated how much he longed for her.

Cruz lost himself in the taste, the feel, the scent of her, convinced that he would never get enough. That he would die from the heated desire that throbbed through his loins, his entire body.

The need for final release was incredibly strong, but that was purely physical. He discovered that his soul longed for something more, for the substance that only being with Savannah could give him.

Raining kisses on her body—her mouth, her throat, her belly—Cruz wove a web of magic that left them both gasping for breath.

Savannah moaned his name, almost delirious with pleasure. Everything within her was vibrating faster than she thought possible. It was as if every moment of their lives had come together to create this moment.

She felt as if she were on fire. Cupping his buttocks, she pulled him to her, kneading his flesh. Her own body felt more aroused than she ever had experienced before.

She was twisting beneath him, making him harden to the point of no return, driving him completely crazy. He had to have her.

Now.

Pulling her to him, Cruz drew his body up the length of hers. Then, as he watched her face, that beautiful face that was forever imprinted on his soul and carried within his heart, he drove himself into her as hard and as deeply as was humanly possible.

Urged on by the thrust of her hips against his, he began to move.

As the rhythm took them to a fever pitch, catapulting them ever higher, Cruz never took his eyes off hers.

And when finally he felt the release, felt her moan his name against his lips, he knew that nothing else truly mattered in this world or any other but this woman he had been allowed to love.

Her heart was hammering wildly against his. The rhythm of his own was just as pronounced, just as wild.

It was exactly like the first time they were together, echoing the moment when they'd both secretly fallen in love. Except better.

He knew it couldn't last, wouldn't last, but while it did, he savored the long moments of bliss as he held her close.

The descent inevitably came, clawing at his euphoria and pulling it away.

Out of his grasp.

He felt like mourning.

Cruz slid off her. He felt her heart still hammering hard against his chest a second before he moved away. It gave him a little hope to cling to.

She nestled against him, as if they were back home, in their own bed. As if she hadn't walked away from him, taking his son.

Taking his pride.

Shutting the thought away, he tried to live only in the moment.

He couldn't bring himself to draw away from her. Not yet. And something inside of him hoped that perhaps this was a sign of things to come. A sign that the worst was over.

That they were husband and wife again.

Sighing, trying vainly to catch her breath, Savannah turned toward him. There was an ache inside of her, an ache that had nothing to do with the man she loved, or with what had just happened here. She'd felt a slight twinge of it earlier. With effort, she forced herself to ignore the budding pain. She didn't want anything to mar what had just happened.

All she wanted to concentrate on was that Cruz had come back to her. That they could be a family again and she could stop feeling so miserably alone.

She feathered her fingers along the slope of his waist. His skin was bronzed in comparison to hers. She always looked like Snow White beside him, she mused. She was so glad that their son had the same golden skin tones that Cruz did.

There was mischief in her eyes as she said, "I guess it's like riding a bicycle. You never quite forget."

Taking her hand, he threaded her fingers through his. "It hadn't been that long."

If you counted it in minutes, in seconds, it was, she thought. And then she laughed. "To a fruit fly, it's been a lot more than several lifetimes."

He wondered if that was her way of starting a discussion about what had driven them apart. Or was it just a subtle recrimination that he hadn't been attentive enough to her needs? That he put the ranch first and that it tired him out too much to be the husband he should have been?

Even though he tried not to let it, he could feel Savannah's words making the hairs on the back of his neck stand up.

Cruz sat up and dragged a hand through his hair before swinging his legs off the bed. It amazed him how carried away he had gotten. Logic had fled from his brain. In a way he felt almost ashamed of himself to have been governed by his emotions, by the physical side of him. He'd thought he'd outgrown that.

"To one of those sea turtles that live to be over a hundred," he pointed out defensively, "it's a blink of an eye."

She detected a warning note in his voice and felt herself stiffening. No, she told herself. They'd just made love together. That was a sign things were getting better. Wasn't it? She cleared her throat. "I guess it's all in the perspective."

"Guess so." His voice was flat, emotionless.

Savannah drew the comforter to her, covering herself, suddenly feeling very naked and exposed. She didn't like what she was hearing in his voice, didn't like that sinking sensation that was taking hold of her stomach.

Had Cruz come here tonight just because he felt a physical need, and being with her was easier than going off to town with the ranch hands and picking up someone?

She had to know the truth, no matter how bitter it was. "Why did you come here?"

He looked at her sharply over his shoulder. Was she telling him that she would have preferred he hadn't come to see her tonight?

But she'd been so warm, so pliant only a few moments ago....

Maybe she was having regrets, he thought. Regrets because she hadn't remained strong, held fast against him. He didn't want to be here to see that. Didn't want to hear Savannah say something that would ruin what had just happened between them.

"Well, it wasn't because the car lost its way," he quipped, not answering her question. Picking up his clothes from where they'd fallen on the floor during their mutual striptease act, he began getting dressed.

Even though the comforter was pulled over her body, Savannah felt horribly naked. She watched as he tugged on his jeans, stuffing his underwear into his pocket. "What are you doing?"

For a second, while he slipped on his shirt, he didn't answer her. "Getting dressed."

She'd thought, hoped, that he would spend the night. Everything until these last few moments had pointed to it. She felt a horrible pang seizing her. From somewhere within, she found her courage.

"Are you leaving?"

He was going because he didn't want to see regret in her eyes. He didn't want to feel like a fool. But all she had to do was ask him to stay and he would. "Do you want me to?"

She wasn't going to beg, wasn't going to ask him to stay when he wanted to leave. There was no triumph in that.

"I don't want you to do anything you don't want to."

He stood looking at her, weighing her words, wishing she'd tell him to stay. But he couldn't force his wishes on her.

And she wasn't saying anything.

He finished buttoning up his shirt. "Then I guess I'm leaving."

She felt her heart shredding. "Why did you come here?" she demanded again.

Without a word, Cruz crossed to the door. At the last moment, he turned back to look at her. He longed to strip off his clothes and make love to her all over again, but seeing her and knowing that there was this wall between them hurt too much.

To save his crumbling pride, to keep from throwing himself at her feet and begging her to end all this nonsense, to take him back before he lost his mind, Cruz stonily replied, "Damned if I know."

He walked out, shutting the door behind him.

Between them.

Savannah got the message, loud and clear. Cruz didn't want to be with her. He didn't want to stay the night now that he no longer craved her sexually. The thought throbbed through her head that she was nothing more than some kind of a release valve to him.

It was as if someone had taken a knife and plunged it into her heart.

If he loved her, he would have remained. To talk. To straighten things out.

To just hold her until the night faded into the past and daylight came to swallow up the shadows.

Now she felt as if there was a huge shadow over her soul.

Unable to hold back any longer, Savannah drew her knees up, buried her face against them and cried.

Thirteen

Cruz blinked, wiping the sweat from his forehead with the back of his gloved hand, wondering if he was seeing things.

The faded red car was still there.

He'd just happened to look in the general direction of the house while leading Diablo around the corral. The last time he'd turned that way, the driveway had been empty. Now it wasn't. The faded red Mustang, the first car he'd ever owned, the one he'd kept alive over the years thanks to creative tinkering and body parts he'd found in junk-yards, was there.

In his driveway. Just as it always had been before Savannah had taken the light from his world.

From out of nowhere, excitement bubbled up like an untapped oil well, filling all the spaces inside of him as if he'd been hollow up to this point.

Oblivious to everything but the horse he'd been training, Cruz looked around to see where his men were. Whistling for Hank's attention, he beckoned to him. "Here, take over."

Even with one arm in a sling, Hank managed to get over the fence with the agility of a cat. He stared at Cruz, dumbfounded. Everyone knew that training was Cruz's exclusive domain. He worked with a horse until it was ready, not allowing any of them to do anything beyond the standard care and feeding.

This was something really different. Especially with this horse, Cruz's favorite. Hank crossed to him, still looking befuddled.

"Take over what?"

"Training." Cruz handed him the reins, almost having to tuck them into Hank's hand. "You've been watching me long enough, haven't you?"

"Yes, sure, but…" The grin that came over Hank's long, angular face threatened to all but split it. "I never thought this day'd come."

Cruz was already jumping over the fence. "Yeah, well, don't let it go to your head. Just do what I was doing with him."

He tossed the last words over his shoulder, rushing away from the corral toward the house. He felt like a schoolboy.

As he approached, he quickly scrutinized the vehicle parked haphazardly before the three front steps that led to the wraparound porch. The porch where he and Savannah had sat, making plans, when they were first married.

They hardly sat here anymore, he thought ruefully.

How the hell had life gotten so twisted up? So complicated?

There were a dozen or so other cherry-red, vintage Mustangs in the area, but none he knew of with that particular dent just above the right fender. In the yard now, Cruz glanced at the license plate. The right letters were all there.

His heart pumped harder.

Cruz ran up the front steps, grinning. It was over. This damn spat of theirs was over. He'd known that if he just waited her out, she'd come to her senses. That she'd realize she missed him as much as he missed her.

He threw open the front door, which he only locked at night. "Savannah!" he called. "Savannah, are you in here?"

It was a rhetorical question. He knew she had to be in the house. The car couldn't just appear in his driveway on its own.

Like a child searching for Christmas presents hidden somewhere in the house, Cruz didn't know where to look first.

A quick run to the kitchen yielded no sign of her. He doubled back and called out again, impatience framing each syllable.

"Savannah, where are you?"

A movement at the top of the stairs caught his eye. When he looked up and saw his wife standing there, a suitcase in her hand, the smile on his face froze. The light that had gone on inside of him began to flicker like a candle set down in a draft.

Cruz gripped the banister to anchor himself. His knees suddenly didn't feel as solid as they should. "What are you doing?"

Savannah had spent hours telling herself that she was a fool for hanging on, that Cruz probably didn't even bother thinking of her, much less spend as much time thinking of

her as she did of him. She'd all but put it on the line for
him, and he'd made his choice. He'd chosen the ranch
over her. Over them.

It was time for her to move on with her life.

If only it didn't hurt like a thousand jagged knives tear-
ing away at her flesh. "I came to get more of my things."

He knew he should just stand aside, let her pass. But he
couldn't. As she came to the landing, he took hold of her
wrist.

"Instead of taking your things to Vanessa's, why don't
you just bring yourself to your things?"

She wasn't going to react to that look, that hint of a
smile. That had been her undoing the last time, and look
where it had gotten her. She was a ranch widow. House-
keepers were shown more attention, more recognition than
she was. "I'm leaving you, Cruz."

He made a hissing noise through his teeth, grappling for
control of his temper. "We've already played this scene out,
Savannah, remember?"

She drew her wrist away. If only she could draw her
heart away as easily, she thought. But maybe in time she
could, she counseled herself.

"No, not this version. This time I'm leaving you for
good. Or bad, as the case may be. At any rate, I'm leaving
permanently."

His temper burst out of its confinement. "What the hell
are you talking about, woman? I came over. We made
love."

Big deal, her mind shouted. *Is that all you think there
is? Sex?* God, he'd completely undersold her. Or she'd
undersold herself.

She held up five fingers of one hand, pushing them into

his face. "Five days ago, Cruz. We made love five days ago. You showed up five days ago, and then nothing, not a word, not a phone call in all that time. Nothing."

"I've been busy," he all but shouted, waving a hand in the general direction of the stables and corral. "If you'd been here, you would have seen—"

She would have seen how he put everything else in front of being with her, Savannah concluded silently. She didn't need or want that.

"I don't have to be here to know you don't have time for me."

Cruz was sorely tempted to shake her. But he'd never gotten physical with a woman and he wasn't about to start with the mother of his children. He fisted his hands and shoved them into his pockets.

"Damn it, Savannah, you could have come back. Nobody said you couldn't."

"Come back to what?" she demanded. "The same conditions?"

"To me," Cruz exclaimed. "You could have come back to me."

With nothing resolved? He would have liked that, she thought. But she couldn't hold her tongue any longer. Not feeling the way she did. "Cruz, we can't go on the way we were—"

"There was nothing wrong the way we were," he cried in exasperation. He hit the top of the banister and almost broke his hand. Shoving it back into his pocket, he could feel the pain working its way up his arm. "I was earning a living, you were helping—"

"We weren't together," she insisted. Why did she have to keep spelling it out for him? Didn't he understand? Or was he hoping to wear her down? After all, he needed his bookkeeper back. He was hopeless with numbers.

"If you wanted to be together, all you had to do was open a window. I was right out there. All you had to do was look!" He angrily gestured toward the corral, as if there were no walls in the way.

"That's not together and you know it." He wasn't that thick; she knew he wasn't. She couldn't have fallen in love with him if he had no more brains than a toasted marshmallow. He was just being too stubborn to admit she was right. "I was hoping that if I went away, you'd come to your senses, see what you were letting slip through your fingers." It was a gamble and she'd lost. "But I think you actually liked it better this way. You were free to be with your mistress as long as you wanted."

He stared at her. Had she lost her mind? "What mistress?" he demanded hotly. "Savannah, what are you talking about? There's no other woman." Days on end went by when she was the only female he even spoke to.

He might have been fooling himself; she didn't know. "There's La Esperanza. She's got a lot stronger hold on your affections than I do."

"I *came* to see you," he reminded her, not knowing what else he could do.

"And then you left again," she countered. Left her feeling used. By leaving so abruptly, by not staying the night, he'd siphoned out the joy in her heart. "You didn't come to talk, to say we'd work things out. You came to satisfy some physical urge you had. Once that was over, you were gone."

He couldn't believe what he was hearing. "You're going to sell yourself short like that?"

Savannah's eyes narrowed. She picked up her suitcase again. "Why not? It's obvious that you have."

Incensed, frustrated, Cruz threw up his hands. "Damn it, woman. What do you want me to say? I can't talk to you when you're like this."

She looked at him knowingly. "And why should now be any different from all the other times?"

Part of her was afraid to walk out the door, knowing that this time it would be permanent. And she didn't want a world that was devoid of Cruz. She loved him. But what would staying get her? Nothing. There was nothing to be gained by wavering. They were just going to dance around the same sentiments, with her being the one to give in all the time. She couldn't do that any longer.

Cruz had made his choice. He'd chosen the ranch over her, over their son and unborn child. They all deserved better than that, and she was tired of trying to fight things the way they were. Not if they weren't going to change.

It took two people to create the kind of change they needed.

Squaring her shoulders, she moved past him to the front door.

Stunned, Cruz remained where he was, staring at her back. "I don't know you anymore."

Savannah looked over her shoulder at him one last time. Her heart ached so badly she thought it was going to crack in half.

"Maybe you never did," she told him.

And then she was gone.

Night pressed down against the land, hot and sticky, as uncomfortable as the people who endured it. The threat of rain had hung over them all day, promising not relief but even worse conditions when the pregnant clouds finally emptied.

The lightning came first, to herald the event. It lit up the sky for a split second, flaming forks of gold that pierced the ground, followed by rolls of thunder.

And the rain continued to hover, the very air tasted of it, but still it wouldn't come.

Cruz had been up half the night, his windows open in hopes of finding some sort of relief, from the weather if not from his tormented state.

She was gone. She was really gone.

Damn it, what was he supposed to do? Crawl? Beg? If he were a rancher like one of the Fortunes, he'd have more than enough people to pick up any slack there might be. Then he could take his family on vacations, on long, languid trips. They could talk all night, play all day.

But he wasn't a Fortune, he was a Perez. And that meant long, hard hours to make ends meet. Someday he could do the things Savannah wanted, but not now. Not yet.

He hated missing her.

Hated not feeling whole.

Finally, Cruz fell into a restless, fitful sleep where reality and dreams became one and the same. He was too exhausted to differentiate between them as they preyed on his mind, haunting him.

They brought his worst nightmare.

Savannah, leaving him. Over and over again. Saying she'd made a mistake in wasting her time loving a man like him.

And then she disappeared, along with everything else. His ranch, his life, it was all gone. And he was left with nothing.

The crash of thunder vibrated in his mind first.

As it grew in volume, it mingled with the high-pitched cries of the horses. The sound was a horrible shriek that, once heard, could never be completely erased from one's mind.

It echoed through his being, followed by a flash of light that made it seem as if the whole world had been set on fire.

Jolting upright, Cruz realized that this wasn't part of his nightmare. This was real. The horses were shrieking.

And then he saw why.

His heart stopped in his chest.

There were flames shooting up from the stable closest to the house. The structure was on fire. One of the bolts of lightning had struck it.

And the horses were inside.

Pulling on his jeans, Cruz grabbed his boots and flew down the stairs.

As he tore out of the back of the house, he could see Jaime and Hank running from the trailer. There was no need to shout orders. Everyone knew that the first priority was to save the horses. Cruz had twenty-nine now, counting the colts and nursing mares. Half were housed in this stable.

Pulling a bandanna from his pocket, he tied it over his nose. He was going to need both hands to gentle the horses and lead them out. There was nothing they were more afraid of than fire.

"If they won't come out," he shouted to Jaime and Hank, "cover their eyes."

The heat felt as if it was singeing his skin even at this distance. Steeling himself, he dived into the inferno.

The flames were in the rear of the stable, but they would eat their way through in a matter of minutes. He had no time to spare. Cruz threw a bridle over one of the mares, then leaped onto the back of another, leading them both out. He turned them loose in the corral before running back inside.

Just as he entered, another terrifying flash of lightning came, creasing the brow of an angry sky. This time, the bolt appeared to be miles away. It ushered in the rain.

On the back of another horse, leading two more out, Cruz took a deep breath and squeezed his eyes shut for just a moment. He could have fallen to his knees in gratitude. There was no need to call the fire department, no need to run for the hoses normally used for filling buckets to wash the animals. The rains had come, and with them, relief. Not from the heat or the stickiness, but from something far worse. From the fire.

The flames sizzled in angry protest as they wove and ducked and were finally vanquished.

After about ten terrifying minutes, the crisis was over. Cruz stood there with his horses, trying to regulate his breathing, taking in the damage.

It might have been one mother of a nightmare, had it not been for the spooked horses.

And the damage.

Cruz slid off the quarter horse, handed the reins over to Jaime and moved forward. The rain lashed his naked chest, plastered his jeans against him and stung his eyes and face as he surveyed what the lightning had done.

The horses would cost him time. They'd been badly spooked and it would be a struggle to get them back to where they'd been only this afternoon. He knew he'd have to work hard. But that was all right. With Savannah gone, there was nothing else but work for him. He was up to it.

He made his way around to the back, to where the rain was mingling with the ashes, making mud. Making despair. No amount of hard work would bring him the money he needed to fix the part of the stable that had been destroyed by the fire. Not immediately, which was when he needed to begin repairs.

Deprived of his wife and son, and with his ranch sustaining a hit, Cruz was beginning to identify very strongly with Job in the Bible.

This was what it had to feel like, coming up against insurmountable odds.

Dragging his hand through his hair, sending the last wave of water flying, Cruz strode back to see to the horses.

Morning did nothing to lift Cruz's mood. Granted, no animals had been lost and the damage could have been a great deal worse, but that didn't minimize the fact that there was damage—damage he needed to fix.

But there was no money to help him fix it. Not for a while. Because he'd paid cash for the four horses he'd bought to train and sell, plus the extra horse he'd picked up, his finances were strapped to the limit.

One of the local ranchers, Nathan Purdue, was coming to look over Cruz's prize stallion, Maximillian, in order to consider paying stud fees for the animal. But even at a thousand dollars or so, that would hardly put a dent in the amount he needed.

Maybe his dream needed to be reconsidered.

No, damn it, this was what he'd wanted since he was five years old. Since he'd "communicated" with his first horse. This was who he was. If this was taken from him, then he had no frame of reference any longer.

With a sigh, he headed for the second stable. For lack of a better plan, they'd doubled up the horses in each stall, but close quarters were not always advisable, even under the best of circumstances.

As he approached the building, he heard a vehicle behind him. A very small part of him thought it might be Savannah experiencing a change of heart.

God, he hoped so. He could do with a friendly face at this point.

But when he swung around to look, he saw that the friendly face belonged to Vanessa, not his wife.

Leaving her car parked askew in the driveway, Vanessa quickly made her way toward Cruz. Unable to stand it any longer, she had made up her mind late last night to meddle in her friends' affairs. The two of them needed to come to their senses and make up. If ever two people belonged together, Cruz and Savannah did. Vanessa had damn well had enough of remaining on the sidelines.

She was so focused on her mission, the prevailing scene only penetrated when she was several feet away from the damaged portion of the stable. The smell of burned, wet wood was almost sickening.

Her eyes wide, she looked at Cruz. "What happened here?" she cried.

He shrugged. "The wrath of God, maybe." He sighed, running his hand through his hair. "The storm last night decided to have an impromptu barbecue, using my stable for wood."

Vanessa slowly walked around the perimeter. From the front, it didn't look so bad. "Well, at least part of it's standing."

He frowned at her cheerful tone. Just like Savannah, he thought. Except that he couldn't muster up his wife's optimism. "Yeah."

Vanessa had already made up her mind on the drive over that if money was the chief obstacle to her friend's happiness she was prepared to lend it to them. Hell, she'd shove it down Cruz's throat if she had to.

Crossing her arms, she walked back to the most damaged part of the stable.

"How much are you going to need to get back on your feet?" she demanded. "Ten thousand? Forty? Help me out here, Cruz. I'm not good at estimates the way Savannah is."

His expression darkened. "Are you offering to lend me money?"

Damn his pride, anyway, she thought. "That's the general idea."

Because she was a friend and meant well, he bit back the first words that rose to his lips, instead saying tersely, "I don't need your money."

She inclined her head, allowing his comment. To an extent.

"Well, maybe not my money, but you're damn well going to need someone's money, and why shouldn't it be mine? At least you know I wouldn't charge you a high rate of interest. To me you're not a risk. A lending institution might not see it that way, but then they don't know you the way I do." He began turning away and she grabbed his arm, forcing him to listen. "Look, if you don't feel strapped, I think you and Savannah can get back to the business of loving each other instead of sparring with each other the way you're doing right now. You're making three people miserable. Four once the baby's born."

He didn't like people meddling in his affairs, even people he liked. "I'm not going to borrow from friends, Vanessa."

"It's a hell of a lot better than borrowing from an enemy." And then she grew serious. "Stop being so wrapped up in yourself that you won't give anyone the pleasure of helping you. Damn your pride, Cruz." She tried to second-guess what was on his mind. "What, are you afraid that if you borrow money from me, that makes you less of a man? Don't you realize that a real man is confident enough to allow his friends to help him when he needs it?" She wasn't getting through to him. "If *I* needed money, would you help me?"

It was a stupid question, on a lot of counts. "You know I would."

"So why can't I help you?" His expression told her she knew why. Vanessa was not about to give up. "Is it because my name is Fortune and yours is Perez? I didn't take you to be the kind of man who allowed himself to be governed by prejudice."

She'd hit him exactly where it hurt. "It's not prejudice."

She crossed her arms again, looking at him knowingly. "Then what would you call it?"

He sighed, defeated. "Okay, maybe I'd call it prejudice."

The smell of victory was beginning to overpower the smell of burned wood. "Ugly word."

Cruz nodded. "Yeah, it is."

"So it's settled?" She put out her hand to seal the bargain.

He took it tentatively, not shaking it yet. "How much interest?"

"The only payment I want over and above the funds I'm

lending you is for you and Savannah to get back together again."

He laughed shortly. "Does your father know you're such a poor businesswoman?"

"I'm an excellent businesswoman, and if my father knew, he'd be cheering me on. Now, are the terms agreeable to you?"

Cruz inclined his head. "I'm willing."

She detected a lack of enthusiasm. "No, you're not. You're willing to have Savannah walk back into the space she vacated. She wants more from you. And she deserves more from you. You know I'm right."

His natural stubborn streak refused to allow him to agree. But all he'd lived with these last two weeks was his stubborn streak, and it was a hell of a less pleasing companion than Savannah had ever been. "Yeah, I do."

"Okay, come back with me to my house and tell her that." When he looked over his shoulder toward the corral, Vanessa cried, "Damn it, Cruz, she was serious about leaving you. When I left her she was calling a divorce lawyer."

The news hit him like a two-by-four against his skull. "What?"

"You heard me. A divorce lawyer. She was crying at the time. Said that hanging around, hoping you'd come back to her, was killing her inside."

He hated being the source of Savannah's pain. Hated, too, that it had taken someone else to make him see the light. "Okay, let me take care of a few things here and I'll follow you."

"Cruz—"

"I swear, I'll be right behind you."

She looked at him dubiously, then finally relented. "Seeing as you had a fire last night, I'll let you off the hook for now. I'll go home and tell Savannah to expect a penitent husband to be paying a call."

He opened his mouth to protest the picture of him she'd just painted, then realized that it was a far more accurate one than anything he could have presented. "Yeah, you tell her that. And tell her I love her."

"Tell her yourself." Vanessa began heading back toward her car, then stopped. "I'll transfer the funds as soon as I get home."

"You don't know my bank account number," he protested.

"Neither do you, probably. Savannah can help me with that. And don't worry about the sum," she said, anticipating his next words, since they hadn't settled on an amount. "It'll more than cover things. I promise."

"Savannah, cancel the divorce lawyer," Vanessa called out the moment she entered the house. "The mountain is coming to see the prophet."

Her voice seemed to echo back to her. The house was eerily quiet.

Strange, she thought. Savannah was usually in the living room, pacing.

On a hunch, Vanessa went to check on Luke in the playroom, then in the entertainment room. Both were empty.

"Savannah, are you in your room?" Even as she called out the question, she hurried to check for herself.

The door was closed. As she approached, she thought he heard the sound of sobbing coming from inside the room. "Savannah, is everything all right?"

Of course it wasn't. Savannah thought she was getting a divorce. Vanessa jeered at her own stupidity. She didn't bother to knock, but opened the door. "Honey's, it's going to be all—"

She stopped dead.

It wasn't Savannah whom she'd heard crying. It was Luke.

The boy was on his knees on the floor, holding his mother's hand, pressing it against his small cheek. Savannah was unconscious.

There was blood on the rug beside her.

Fourteen

Cruz meant to follow Vanessa within a few minutes, he really did.

But one thing came on the heels of another and he got caught up situating the horses. Temporary accommodations had been made, but he knew he was borrowing trouble, stabling two horses to a stall. Granted, it was summer and the animals could stay out, but he preferred keeping them indoors at night. This area wasn't without wolves and bobcats, not to mention rattlesnakes. He wanted no surprise night visitors for his horses.

Taking out his credit card, one of the first things he'd signed up for when he'd finally bought his own place, Cruz handed the card to Billy.

"I want you to go into town and get me enough lumber to board up the back of the stable." It would be a temporary fix, until he could get Ike Cannon and his son, Russ, to come out and give him an estimate. He could repair the place himself, but the way things were right now, it would mean doing without sleep for the next month.

A man could only do so much. There came a time when he had to let go a little. Cruz figured his time was at hand.

Taking off his hat, Billy scratched his head as he surveyed the damaged portion. "Gonna take a lot to rebuild that."

"Yeah, I know. Right now I just want to put up some boards to keep the horses from getting out at night—or anything else from getting in. Now vamoose." He did a quick calculation. Savannah couldn't turn him down after what had happened last night. She loved the ranch as much as he did. He'd make his case with her and bring her and Luke home within the hour. "I should be back by the time you return from town."

But as he began to walk toward where the vehicles were parked, Billy called out, "What about Purdue? You want me to tell Hank to send him away when he comes?"

Cruz stopped in midstep.

"Damn, I forgot about Purdue. No, we can't afford to send him away." Even as he spoke, he saw the man's black SUV in the distance.

Business before pleasure.

Not that he saw going at it with Savannah as pleasure. Funny how stubborn she seemed to have become lately, Cruz thought. Or was that streak always there and he hadn't noticed it before?

Taking out his cell phone, he was about to call Vanessa to make his apologies and ask her to explain the situation to Savannah. He didn't want to lose his wife, but if he allowed things to slide, he'd have no ranch to bring her home to. No way to provide for her and their children. What kind of a life would that be? He needed to stay and talk with Purdue before the fickle rancher took his stud money and his influence elsewhere.

As Cruz flipped open the silver phone, it rang in his hand.

"Hey, that's a neat trick. How'd you do that?" Billy asked, peering over his shoulder at the cell phone.

Cruz waved a hand at him to be quiet as he pressed a button and placed the device to his ear. Even as he did so, he braced himself. He never got calls on the cell, unless they were from Savannah. But this one was from Vanessa, no doubt calling to get on his case, too.

"Look," he immediately began, feeling defensive, "I got a little behind, but—"

"Well, you'd better get your behind here now."

There was something in her voice that told him she wasn't just calling to upbraid him about being late. Something that made his gut tighten. "What's wrong?"

"I'm at the hospital."

"Hospital?" Visions of Luke flying off the roof, the way he had already once attempted, flashed through Cruz's mind. That time, luckily, he'd seen what the boy was up to and had raced to catch him. He'd barely made it. But this time, he hadn't been there to catch his son. "What happened to Luke?"

"Nothing—"

"Nothing?" he interrupted. "Then why—"

She didn't let him finish framing his question. "It's Savannah."

Cruz felt as if he'd just been kicked in the stomach by the same stallion whose fees he was about to negotiate. A hundred possibilities crowded into his head, one thought being interrupted by the next until they were all jumbled in his head.

His mouth felt like cotton. His tongue stuck to the roof of his mouth. "Why? What's happened to her?"

Vanessa had no real answer for that, at least not yet. She gave it her best guess.

"Cruz, it's the baby. I found Savannah on the floor in her room, unconscious. She was bleeding. I'm not sure—" Emotion choked off her words, making it impossible to finish.

Savannah was stronger than she looked, he told himself silently. Everyone thought Savannah was so frail, but she wasn't. He grasped that thought and hung on to it. "Is she conscious?"

There was a long pause on the other end of the line. He felt his gut shredding. "No."

Fear tightened the bands around his heart several more degrees, making it almost impossible for him to breathe. "Which hospital?" She gave him the name. It was the same one he'd taken Hank to. "I'll be right there."

Feeling like a man trapped inside a nightmare, he slipped the phone back into his breast pocket.

Even as Cruz turned toward the car, he saw Purdue walking toward him, a large, expansive smile on his face. When he reached him, the big man rubbed his hands together.

"I'm ready to make some babies, Perez. Long as the price is right."

Cruz didn't want to send Purdue away. The man's ego was the kind that would cause him to take his business elsewhere if he felt the least bit slighted. And his business was important to Cruz. It didn't represent just a single event. If Purdue was pleased with the stud, there were over a dozen other ranchers who tended to follow his lead, and that meant business would pick up just when he needed it most.

But he couldn't stand here and negotiate stud fees while his own wife lay unconscious at the hospital. He needed to be with her in case—

He needed to be with her, he amended, refusing to take the thought any further than that.

"I'm afraid there's been a slight change of plans, Mr. Purdue."

Bushy eyebrows came together over a nose that had been broken twice before the man had reached the age of puberty. "Change of plans? Look, if you're trying to play hard to get, Perez, it's not going to work. Maximillian's got great lines, but he's not the only stallion in the stable. I can always—"

Cruz didn't have time to hear the man go on and on. "I'm not trying to play hard to get, Mr. Purdue. My wife's just been taken to the hospital. I'm on my way there now." He made up his mind. "But I've got a man who can negotiate the fees with you." Turning, he beckoned Hank over from the corral. "Hank!"

Hank's long legs brought him over quickly. "Yeah, Boss?"

Cruz put his arm confidently on Hank's shoulder. "Mr. Purdue, this is my foreman, Hank Jeffers. He knows everything I do about La Esperanza. Hank, I want you to negotiate Maximillian's stud fees for me. I've got to get to the hospital to see Savannah."

Hank looked at Cruz uncertainly. Turning away from

the burly older rancher, he lowered his voice and asked, "When did I become foreman?"

"Two minutes ago. Now take care of this for me." Cruz gave Purdue a forced smile, then hurried over to Billy, who was still standing by the truck, watching what was transpiring with the awe of a child. "Billy, give me the keys to your car. I want you to take my truck to get the lumber."

The cowboy dug out his keys and handed the ring to Cruz, taking the keys to the pickup. Jumping into the cab, he was gone in a matter of seconds.

Cruz hardly remembered what he said to Purdue in parting. He knew he didn't give any extra advice to Hank, but he was pretty sure the young man would come through.

He was just going to have to trust Hank, he thought, pushing down hard on the gas pedal.

After he'd put a few miles between himself and the ranch, he realized his hands were shaking as he clutched the steering wheel. He also realized that he'd never, ever been so scared in his life. Not even when he'd gotten lost as a boy when he'd gone camping with his family. He'd spent the night huddled at the mouth of a cave, shivering and praying for daylight.

Now he was praying for something a whole lot more nebulous. Daylight always came. But the uncertainty of what he was facing, of what Savannah was facing, threatened to do him in. He had the feeling that he was praying for a miracle. But he didn't know how. Miracles didn't occur for people like him.

He didn't have Savannah's ability to think positively.

Savannah.

Damn it, why had he allowed all this to happen? Why hadn't he given her the time she deserved? She was the best thing that had ever happened to him and he damn well knew it. From the first time he'd taken her in the stable, making love with her had felt like some kind of out-of-body experience. It had never felt like that with any other woman. Memories pushed forward, taking hold of him, making him feel what he'd felt then.

Like a high-speed train, those memories instantly carried him back over five years ago, until once again he was in the Double Crown stable.

In his memory he stood away from the stall, watching Savannah's face as he allowed her closer access to Hellfire. The golden quarter horse that had given him so much trouble in the beginning had won a special place in his heart and was now his personal favorite. Vanessa had presented Hellfire to him on his twenty-fifth birthday. He'd never had a gift, before or since, that he'd loved nearly half as much.

Cruz liked the reverent admiration he saw in Savannah's face when she looked at the animal. "Well, what do you think?" he asked her.

Murmuring words of endearment, Savannah gently ran her hand along the horse's muzzle, stroking it. "I think she's beautiful."

Leaning against the stall, Cruz laughed. "It's a he, not a she. You can tell the difference by—"

Obviously flustered, she flushed with color and stepped away. She lowered her eyes and looked more closely at the horse.

"Yes," she said quickly, making Cruz want to laugh, "I know exactly how to tell the difference. I was raised on a ranch." His laughter brought a deepening color to her cheeks that he found fascinating. "Don't laugh at me."

Guiding her away from Hellfire, Cruz drew her toward an empty stall. "Oh, but I'm not laughing at you, I'm laughing at how impossibly sweet and innocent you seem."

Stung, she raised her chin in protest. "I'm not innocent."

Because she denied it, he began to think that, just possibly, it wasn't an act. That she really *was* an innocent. His laughter melted into a wide, sensuous smile. "Oh, excuse me. But of course you're very worldly."

She shrugged, looking away. "Well, all right, not very, but—"

He placed his hands on her shoulders, drawing her attention back to him and the moment. The protest died on her lips.

The wide smile was gone, replaced by a smaller, more intense one as he regarded her. She was easily one of the most beautiful women he'd ever seen. Beautiful and innocent. The combination was irresistible. With the tip of his finger, he toyed with a wisp of her hair that fell against her cheek.

"And as a worldly woman, you wouldn't be offended if I kissed you."

"If you what?" she whispered.

He found the confusion in her eyes unexpectedly sweet, and arousing. His hands tightened ever so slightly on her shoulders as he brought her closer to him. "I prefer showing to talking."

Cruz slipped his hands up along the sides of her throat until his fingers gently framed her face. He felt the excitement growing within him, vibrating with every beat of his heart.

Waiting.

Anticipating.

She melted against him the moment his lips touched hers, a snowflake unable to keep its shape when it was blown into the path of a sunbeam.

The moan that escaped her lips was the sound of surrender.

Hearing her, tasting the moan on his tongue, aroused Cruz to a fever pitch he'd never encountered before. It took effort to slow his progress.

He thrived on conquests, enjoyed giving the rich ladies what they wanted while they pretended not to—a wild tumble with the rough hired help. He enjoyed them even as he knew they were using him to supply a much sought-after thrill and a story to tell. That was where he derived his pleasure—from knowing exactly what they were, exactly what they were after. And he knew enough not to become emotionally entangled in what his body was doing.

But Savannah's kiss was oddly innocent for all the preconceived notions he had brought to this moment of seduction. So innocent that it made him pause for the slightest instant.

The next moment, there was something else in its place. Something that snatched him up even when he had no intention of being captured.

The same innocence that he'd wondered at had thrown a lariat over him, ensnaring him as easily as a fleeing colt. The questing wonder within Savannah's kiss, coupled with the growing hunger he detected, took him prisoner, so much so that he thought of resisting because of the overwhelming effect it brought in its wake. But then he gave up the notion, deciding to enjoy the moment.

Or he thought he decided.

If he were being honest with himself, he would have admitted that the decision had been taken out of his hands the moment he felt her soft body molding itself against him. It had been made for him by some outside force that took unending pleasure in watching him get captured in the very trap he laid for others.

Seeking refuge in the lie that he was only taking a busman's holiday, Cruz abandoned all pretense of remaining detached, and allowed himself to be engulfed by the sensations that were already running rampant through him.

He deepened the kiss, assaulting her mouth again and again. With each pass he wanted more rather than less. Savannah shivered once as he tugged at the zipper that ran the length of her back. Drawing it all the way down, he felt the dress fall from her body, and then saw by the look in her eyes that he had won her.

Won both her and an additional, unexpected prize. A thrill came to him the way it hadn't in a long, long time, igniting his loins and his soul.

He was unprepared for her.

Cruz was accustomed to women becoming clawing wildcats in his embrace. Accustomed and proud in his own way that he had unveiled this secret about them. That for all their pretenses of polished manners and sophistication, they were just swirling cauldrons of hunger and desire like their poorer sisters.

But he was not accustomed to feeling that he had just crossed the threshold of dewy innocence, helping to let loose a secret that innocence had never suspected existed. Cruz had the very real impression, as he kissed her over and over again, that Savannah was more surprised than he at the depth of her reaction, the breadth of the feelings that were stirred by his artful lovemaking.

And so, in part, the seducer became the seduced, charmed, taken, aroused by the very woman with whom he had chosen to dally.

Very quickly, it ceased to resemble a dalliance in any manner, shape or form. It became, instead, an experience, sweet for all the hot passion that surrounded it. And enduring, for it burned itself into his mind, into his very soul.

Everything melted into everything else. The stable, the horses, the hay within the stall—it all faded from his consciousness. All there was was this woman, this soft flower, who had the ability to reduce him to a mass of molten desire.

He felt almost humbled as he touched her, as he felt her body heat beneath his hand. This was new and different, yet it seemed as if he'd been waiting for her all his life. As if he'd known her all his life.

Each place he touched her quivering body seemed a revelation to him, leaving him anticipating, yearning.

She became a wild woman beneath his questing mouth. It was as if every fiber of her had caught on fire and only he could put it out.

But he didn't put it out. With each movement, he only fed it, making it rise higher.

With practiced skill, Cruz moved his fingers, his lips and his tongue over her body, teaching her about herself, showing her that there was no place, no tiny spot, that was immune to him, to the wonders of lovemaking. They were all centers of passion.

The skin behind her knees, the space inside her elbow, the hollow of her throat, all these he teased, all these he turned into places of heated desire. And when he moved to where all things came together, when he finally drove himself into her, the excitement barely allowed him to breathe.

Cruz roused himself, shaking his head and steadying his breath, which was made erratic by the mere memory of his first night with Savannah. Now wasn't the time to let his mind wander.

He couldn't lose her. He couldn't. Losing her would be like losing the other half of his soul.

"Hang on, baby," he said aloud, hardly aware that he was doing so. "You've got to hang on so I can make it up to you."

Tears came, clouding his vision. He wiped them away with the back of his sleeve. A light in the rearview mirror caught his eye just as he heard the sound of a siren.

He blinked, trying to focus. There were dancing red, yellow and blue lights on the car behind him.

A police car.

Somehow, he'd crossed into the city limits without even realizing it. And he'd obviously exceeded the speed limit without realizing it, too.

A sense of urgency pushed him on. Cruz wanted nothing more than to ignore the squad car behind him, but he knew the futility of that. Suppressing an impatient sigh, he pulled over.

Feeling as if each moment was ticking away from him, he waited restlessly, watching in the side mirror as the officer left his vehicle and made his way up to Billy's car.

Gabe Thunderhawk was taking a well-deserved break from the investigation. And from Detective Andrea Matthews, who was rubbing him the wrong way, so hard he felt as if his skin was abraded.

He needed to clear his head.

When the dusty navy-blue car with its broken taillight had gone whizzing by him, he'd thought he was dreaming. No one drove that fast past a police car.

Nobody but a punk kid thumbing his nose at authority. Red Rock didn't lack for those.

So he'd given chase. After a couple of blocks, he'd had to sound his siren because the damn fool refused to slow down.

Taking out his ticket book, he pushed his hat back on his head, ready for anything.

"Okay, so where's the fire— Cruz?" Surprised, Gabe took a second look at the car he'd just stopped. He was familiar with both of Cruz's vehicles and this wasn't one of them. "This isn't your car."

"No, it belongs to one of my ranch hands." There was no time to get into explanations about the fire or why Billy needed Cruz's truck and he needed Billy's wreck. He couldn't push away the feeling that every moment counted. That if he didn't hurry, it might be too late. Damn it, why hadn't he gone with Vanessa when she'd asked him to? He could already be with Savannah. "Gabe, they just took Savannah to the hospital. I've got to go see her."

All signs of the police officer vanished. They were neighbors now. Friends. Everyone loved Savannah. "Is it serious?"

It killed Cruz to say it. "Yeah." The single word twisted a knife deep into his gut.

Gabe was already rushing back to his squad car. "Hang on, I'll give you an escort in."

Cruz made the rest of the trip in fifteen minutes. With Gabe's "I hope she's okay," ringing in his ears, he tore into the emergency room, ignoring the admitting clerk even as the matronly woman jumped to her feet to stop him. "Sir, you can't just run in there."

"My wife's in there," he said, then called out her name. "Savannah!" He knew he must look like a deranged fool, running around the place calling for her, but he didn't care. It didn't matter. The only thing that mattered was finding Savannah.

And that she was well.

He felt someone catch his arm. When he swung around, he saw that it was Vanessa.

"They just took her up to a room," she told him, even now guiding him toward the bank of elevators. "I was getting her things together to take upstairs." She tried to smile and wasn't very successful. "Your voice carries a long way."

"Is she all right?" He searched Vanessa's face, looking for his answer, hoping he could detect a lie if faced with one.

The elevator came. Vanessa stepped inside and pressed the button for the third floor. He got in with her.

"For now," she told him.

He didn't like the sound of that. Didn't like the way his heart froze in his chest, like a lump of ice. "What do you mean, 'for now'? What's wrong with her? What happened?"

Vanessa sighed. "Savannah's not as strong as she thinks she is. This pregnancy's been harder on her than the first one. I guess her body just gave out."

No, it didn't, he thought. *No, it didn't.* "I want to see her doctor."

"He went up with her. I just left him." She threaded her arm through his and looked at him in surprise. "You're shaking."

Machismo would have had him denying it. But he wasn't feeling very macho. He was feeling like a man who was in danger of losing everything that made the world right to him.

"Never felt so cold before," he admitted.

"It's going to be all right," Vanessa promised.

The elevator doors opened. The fog enshrouding his brain lifted as he stepped off the elevator. "Where's Luke?"

"He's okay," she assured him. "I left him with my housekeeper. I called your mother after I talked to you. She's on her way to him right now."

He nodded. "Good."

Better that his mother went to Luke than came here, he thought. He wasn't sure that he could remain strong if his mother began to show him any sympathy. All that was holding him together right now was the steely grit he'd wrapped around himself the moment Vanessa had called.

The steel shattered when he walked into Savannah's room and saw her.

His wife was unconscious. There were tubes running into her arm. He'd never seen her look this pale and fragile.

Why hadn't he seen this coming? Why hadn't he realized that she was working too hard? That this was too much for her right now?

Because he was never there himself, he thought angrily. And when he was, he'd let her wait on him, serve him as if he was some kind of dictator, or self-absorbed Neanderthal. He'd been so tired, he hadn't noticed how worn out she was.

Hell of a husband he made, he thought.

The doctor was nowhere to be seen. When he asked Vanessa his whereabouts, she said, "I'll go find him."

Cruz was barely conscious of nodding. Walking farther into the room, he took Savannah's hand in his. "Wake up, baby. Please wake up."

But Savannah didn't even stir.

What if she didn't wake up? If she never woke up?

The fear inside him grew to almost unmanageable proportions.

His knees weak, Cruz sank onto the chair beside Savannah's bed, still holding her hand.

Fifteen

Cruz jumped to his feet the second Dr. Miller walked in. It was almost ten and he hadn't thought the physician was going to make another visit until sometime the next morning.

Cruz's back ached. Tension riddled it, and it didn't help that the chair he'd been sitting in was beginning to feel like a twelfth-century instrument of torture.

He held his breath as the doctor picked up Savannah's medical chart to read the nurses' notations.

Unable to keep silent any longer, Cruz asked, "It's been ten hours. Shouldn't she be waking up by now?"

"Ordinarily, yes." Dr. Miller tucked away the chart at the foot of the bed. "But sometimes the body knows best." The physician regarded his patient for a long moment before glancing at Cruz again. "Your wife's been through a great deal. Look at it this way. Her body is making an attempt to rally, to 'get back to normal,' so to speak. If she's not conscious, her body's not focusing on anything else but getting better."

"But she is getting better, right?" Cruz pressed.

Miller had given him a complete prognosis earlier, when he'd first arrived, but he needed to hear it again. Needed to be assured that Savannah was going to be all right. He knew there were no guarantees, but he still needed something to hang on to. Even a lie.

"Yes." With an understanding nod, Dr. Miller reviewed what he'd already told him, stripping away the technical jargon. "We've given your wife something to stop her from going into premature labor. At present, it appears that the baby was unaffected by this episode." He glanced at Savannah. "She just needs to come around." And then he laid a compassionate hand on Cruz's shoulder. "There's no telling how long that's going to take. Why don't you go home, Mr. Perez? I can have someone call you the moment your wife opens her eyes."

Cruz blew out a long breath, looking at Savannah and willing her to do just that. "I am home, Doctor. She's my home. There's no place else I can be."

Miller had heard the words before, coming from other spouses. But it didn't negate the reality of the situation. "You need your rest."

Cruz pressed his lips together, looking at Savannah. He tried not to let his imagination get the better of him. He'd never been able to hang on to sunny thoughts. That was Savannah's department. "Everything I need is right there in that bed, Doctor."

It was clear that there was no room for argument or debate. With a nod, the physician patted his shoulder. "I'll be by again in the morning."

Cruz turned on his heel as Miller began to leave the room. "The morning? What if she needs you in the middle of the night?"

The doctor paused by the door. "I've got a very competent colleague on standby. And the nurses on staff are the best." A small smile slipped across his lips. "I had an opportunity to experience that firsthand last year." He looked at Savannah, then back at Cruz. "If she were my wife, I'd want her here."

"I just want her back on the ranch," Cruz murmured quietly, trying to mask the impatience that ricocheted through him.

"I understand," Dr. Miller replied before he left the room.

Agitated, Cruz began to pace the small space that comprised Savannah's single care unit. He tried not to let his imagination run away with him. Vanessa had left over an hour ago, going home for the night. His parents had both been by, first his father, then his mother, taking turns so that Luke wouldn't be left alone at their house. The boy had been assured that everything was all right, that his mother was just resting, but Rosita had told Cruz that Luke looked unconvinced.

"He's as sharp as you were at that age, Cruz," she'd said when she came to visit. She stood stroking Savannah's head, fighting tears. "You're going to have your hands full with that one."

They already did, he thought. And Savannah handled it. Savannah handled everything at the house. Guilt lanced through him as he considered the list of things his wife faced every day. All without complaining. He hadn't realized how much he relied on her until he'd been left with everything to do. They were behind in the bookkeeping.

Behind in everything.

Restless, frustrated, Cruz moved back to the bed, looking at Savannah's pale face. She hadn't moved since they had brought her up from the emergency room this morning, he'd been told. Hadn't opened her eyes. He'd been right here in this room the entire time, waiting, hoping.

Insisting that he eat something, Vanessa had brought him a sandwich from the cafeteria. It was sitting on the shelf by the window, still wrapped in cellophane. But he had no appetite.

He had nothing without Savannah.

Oh God, what if—?

Taking her hand, he got down on his knees beside her bed. He searched for the words with which to pray, but he couldn't remember how.

After a moment, he addressed his maker. "Yeah, it's me. I know. We haven't talked for a while." He shifted his shoulders, feeling as if there was no way to hide from the pain. From the devastating helplessness that drenched him. "No disrespect intended. It's just that I've been busy. But You already know that." He laughed shortly. "You know everything." Cruz looked up toward the ceiling. "Like the fact that I can't go on without her. I'll do anything You want.

"Anything," he pleaded. "Just please don't take her from me. Make her wake up. I need her, God. I need her a lot more than You do. Make her open her eyes so I can tell her. Please."

He looked at Savannah through his tears, but her eyes didn't open.

With a sigh, Cruz buried his head on the blanket and wept.

* * *

She hurt all over.

The more she struggled to rise to the surface, the more the pain wrapped itself around her, telling her not to struggle, to remain buried where she was.

It was nice here.

Safe.

As long as she remained inside the cocoon with its gauzy walls and its soothing remoteness, she was safe.

There were no demands on her here. No pain, no pressure. No days that fed into one another filled with endless tasks, constant demands that drained her and left her feeling unfulfilled.

But there was no Luke here. No Cruz. And she felt alone.

Ached to be with them.

Summoning strength from some long lost, darkened corner, she struggled against the natural urge to remain safe, secluded. Warm and pain free. She struggled to reach the surface.

To find the people she loved more than life itself.

The sound of words guided her. Cruz's voice, coming to her from a distance…asking her something…telling her something….

Bartering with someone for her life.

Or maybe it was someone else's voice. She wasn't sure. But she told herself it was Cruz, and held on to that possibility as if it were a lifeline. Without it, she knew she would have sunk back to the bottom and remained there indefinitely.

Slowly, like a deep-sea diver avoiding the bends, she rose from the depths. Struggling every endless inch of the way, she made it to the surface. Gritting her teeth, she embraced the pain.

Her eyelids weighed a ton each, but she fought to push them open. Several times, she thought she'd succeeded, only to realize they were still closed.

She tried again and again.

It felt as if the struggle, the battle for survival, took all night.

It drained her beyond words. Still, she fought on.

When she finally managed to open her eyes, daylight had moved into the room, banishing the shadows.

She had no idea where she was. Nothing looked familiar.

Her field of vision expanded slowly. From the tubes that ran into her arms, to the white blanket that covered the bed she was in. To the man sleeping in the chair beside her.

Cruz.

What there was of her heart jumped.

Her throat felt parched. It took effort to make even a single sound.

"Cruz?"

His eyes flew open instantly. He'd heard Savannah's voice calling his name a dozen time during the course of the night.

But each time he looked, her eyes were still shut and she was still unconscious.

But this time was different.

He almost fell to his knees as he grasped her hand. "Savannah, you're awake."

"Of course I'm awake." She cleared her raspy throat. "It's morning." Morning. And she should be doing things. Getting things ready.

But where was she? And where was Luke?

And what was Cruz doing here, with that sad, drawn look on his face?

He closed his hand around hers. "Oh God, baby, you're awake."

"Uh-huh." They'd already established that. She struggled to keep the fog from closing around her again. God, she hurt. She felt as if she'd been run over by a truck, several times. "Wh-what am I doing here?"

"Vanessa said she found you on the floor in your room. You were unconscious." Cruz ran his tongue along his dried lips. Even talking about it sent ripples of fear through him. "There was blood—"

"Blood?" she echoed. The next moment, as the words and their implication penetrated, Savannah struggled to sit up, panicked. "The baby—"

Cruz was on his feet instantly, gently pushing her back and restraining her. Not that it took much effort, for she felt as weak as a kitten.

"The baby is fine," he assured her. "Vanessa had them call in Dr. Miller."

It was Vanessa who had remembered the name of Savannah's OB-GYN. Another category he'd fallen short in. But no more. From here on, everything that affected his wife and his children affected him as well.

"He gave you something to stop the labor." Cruz let out a shaky breath. He looked at her, devouring her with his eyes. She was awake. She was going to be all right, a voice in his head cheered over and over again. "You gave me one hell of a scare."

She tried to force a smile to her lips, but felt as weak as a strand of overcooked spaghetti.

Things began to come together in her mind. She remembered feeling a terrible stab of pain. And then the room going black.

"Wasn't too good from this end, either." Just before she'd passed out, she remembered Luke crying out to her. Fresh panic overtook her. "Luke…?"

"He's with my parents."

Cruz didn't know if she remembered that Luke had been with her at the time, but he saw no need to tell her that now. Knowing Savannah, she'd only blame herself for scaring the boy.

A furrow formed between her eyes. "It's daylight, Cruz. Why…"

He held her hand, feeling as if he never wanted to let go. "Yeah." It was finally daylight, he thought. Daylight for both of them.

"Why are you here?" she asked next. "Why aren't you at the ranch?"

He'd gotten several calls yesterday. Hank had wanted to keep him informed of both the outcome of the negotiation with Purdue and how Billy had fared at the lumberyard. The three hands had spent the better part of the day boarding up the stable, where the horses had been housed with apparently a minimum of fuss last night.

"I left Hank in charge," he told her. It tickled him to see the look of surprise that came over her features. He gave Savannah her due, something he knew he had neglected for far too long. "You were right. He is good. I made him foreman. He's handling the repairs."

"Repairs?" she repeated. As far as she remembered, nothing had needed fixing.

"To the stable." He watched the furrow between her

eyes deepen. "Part of the stable closest to the house burned down."

"Burned down?" Savannah echoed incredulously. She felt as if she'd fallen headfirst into a rabbit hole. "Just how long was I out?"

He moved the hair back from her face, caressing her cheek. Silently, he thanked God for listening, even after such a long separation.

"Too long. Since about ten yesterday," he told her.

Who was this man and where was her husband? she wondered. "And you've been here all that time?"

"Yes."

It didn't make any sense to Savannah—although there was one plausible explanation for it. "Am I dead?"

All the relief he felt was caught up in the laugh that left his lips. "No, baby, but I thought you were going to be." He took her hand again, looking into her eyes. The beautiful eyes that he loved. "It made me realize a whole lot of things. Like nothing is as important to me as you are."

She smiled, not completely convinced she'd been wrong in her assumption. "Maybe I should try being dead more often."

He sobered. "Don't even kid about that." He pressed a kiss to her forehead. "Just get better." Sitting back, Cruz took a breath. "The doctor says you're going to have to cut back on things until the baby comes."

She frowned again. Easy for the doctor to say. She knew that his wife had a housekeeper. "Cut back on things?"

Cruz nodded. "As in 'take it easy.'"

"Take it easy?" The last time she'd done that was right after she'd given birth to Luke. Ever since then her life had been a blur of activity.

He laughed again. "And learn not to repeat everything."

Already working on the problem, she hardly heard him. This was going to take coordination. And cooperation. She was going to have to impose on several people, something she hated doing.

"I guess," she began slowly, "if I stay at Vanessa's house until after the baby's born—"

He stopped her right there. "You're staying on the ranch."

Staying at the ranch was not going to solve the problem. It was going to add to it. Although, she had to admit, the idea of being separated from Cruz any longer was clearly killing her. As the song went, she'd rather be miserable loving him than happy loving anyone else. "But then who's going to help me with Luke?"

"I am." He said it as if there was no doubt he was up to it. And they both knew he wasn't, she thought.

Savannah shook her head. "No, you're already too busy to breathe."

He had been. Until he'd almost lost his very reason *for* breathing.

"You're always telling me that I should learn how to delegate." Sitting down on the edge of the bed beside her, he threaded his fingers through hers. "Besides, with the money Vanessa is lending us, I can get the stable rebuilt and hire on an extra hand. That'll free me up to help you. And my mother and sisters all want to pitch in. You're not going to have to lift a finger—"

Her mind had stopped processing information when he'd casually dropped a key phrase in her lap. "Vanessa is lending us money?"

He realized that in all the excitement he'd forgotten to mention that. "Yes."

The information was just not sinking in. This wasn't Cruz, this was some clone. "And you're letting her," she said slowly.

Cruz nodded. "It's already a done deal."

Savannah looked dubiously at the bottle dripping solution into her veins. "Are you sure I'm not dead?" She turned her eyes back to Cruz. "Or at least still unconscious? Because this is just the kind of hallucination I'd have if I were out of my head."

He laughed softly, shaking his own head. "No hallucination, Savannah. I know I got carried away there for a while, but I realized something last night, sitting here beside you and waiting for you to open your eyes again. That it doesn't matter if I have the best ranch in Texas, not if you're not there to share it with me." He shrugged his shoulders casually, letting them drop again. "Besides, I found out that I kind of like delegating." He thought of the first phone call he'd gotten from his new foreman yesterday. "Hank got an even better stud fee for Maximillian than I was going to ask for. And Purdue is going to recommend us to his friends. We'll be able to pay Vanessa back with interest in no time, even if she doesn't want any."

He was telling Savannah she wasn't dreaming, but it certainly felt like it. She tried very hard to make all the pieces fit.

"So you're really serious? You're going to start spending more time with Luke and me?"

He found it hard not to grin like an idiot. Savannah was talking to him, sounding just like she always had. She was going to be all right. "Never more serious in my life."

Though it was getting clearer, her brain still felt rather foggy. "Were you here last night?"

He raised her hand to his lips and kissed it, grateful to be able to do so. "I've been here ever since Vanessa called to say you were at the hospital. Why?"

Things began falling into place. "Then it was you I heard talking in my sleep."

It was his turn not to understand. "What?"

"When I was unconscious, I thought I heard a voice. I used it to help pull me out of the abyss I was in. I thought it was the voice of God." She smiled at him, her heart overflowing with love. "I guess I made a mistake."

"Not God, just me," he admitted. She'd been unconscious the entire evening and night. He looked at her in surprise. "Then you heard me?"

She nodded, loving him even more than she ever had before. "I heard you. I wasn't conscious, but I heard you." Savannah reached up and touched his face. "I'm sorry about everything."

Turning her hand, he kissed the palm. "You have nothing to be sorry about." And then he amended his words. "Except maybe for marrying a jackass like me."

"That is the one thing I am not sorry about. I love a jackass like you," she told him with a grin.

Cruz moved in closer. "Hold that thought," he advised as he leaned down to kiss her lightly on the lips.

She sighed contentedly. But then he drew back. Her eyes opened and she looked at him. "Is that the best you've got?"

He nodded, trying to appear solemn when everything inside of him was cheering. He'd gotten a second chance. In more ways than one. A second chance to make things right.

"For now, with all these tubes attached to you. Once I get you home, I'll show you my best."

He loved the way her smile began in her eyes. "Something to live for," she said.

Cruz ran his thumb along her lower lip, love shining in his eyes as he looked at her. "Definitely something to live for."

For Savannah, this all felt too good to be true. "And no rain checks?"

He shook his head. "No rain checks," he promised. "I'll show you my best the second you walk through the door."

She longed to put her arms around his neck. For now, though, she had to content herself with the promise of things to come. "Then I guess we'd better leave Luke with your parents."

"Good plan," he agreed.

"Can I have just the tiniest sample?" She held up her thumb and forefinger, gazing at him hopefully.

"Just the tiniest," he allowed. And then he leaned in again to kiss her one more time.

* * * * *

Everything you love about romance...
and more!

Please turn the page for Signature Select™
Bonus Features.

A Baby Changes Everything

Bonus Features:

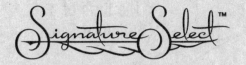

BONUS FEATURES

A Baby Changes Everything

BEHIND THE SCENES
The Birth of a Continuing Series

Recently Marsha Zinberg, Executive Editor, Signature Select Program, took some time out from her busy schedule to answer some questions about continuity books and how they are developed.

4

Who comes up with the idea?

At Harlequin, we use a team approach for generating ideas that can evolve into continuing series. Usually, a group of editors will sit down and put their heads together. They are always on the lookout for ideas that seem "big enough" to be developed into a continuity series. Our inspiration comes from current television shows, films, news stories, magazine articles...anything is fair game! The most promising ideas are given some development by a team, and once we've fleshed out several ideas we're excited about, we test them with our readers to see if they're excited, too. After a decision is made as to which concept to move forward with, the Continuities Team does more work to further develop and refine the concept. Then we're ready to turn it over to our talented authors!

Who chooses the authors?
We select a group of authors to participate in the series, each of whom brings a unique set of creative skills to the project. Since a continuing series is a group effort, it offers a different dynamic for many authors, who are used to working in isolation and nurturing their books very much on their own. Writing is usually a very lonely business! So the authors we select have to be comfortable working as part of a creative unit consisting of other authors and the editorial team. In addition, the editorial team tries to match the subject matter and genre of the particular book within the series to the authors' individual writing styles, habits and areas of expertise. We would not ask an author beloved for her Western stories to participate in a series set in the glitzy New York City social scene, nor would we ask an author known for her romantic suspense stories to give us a big family drama!

Are there guidelines? How can the authors keep everything straight?
In order to avoid total chaos, we create a document known as a bible (just as they do for the writers of television series), which gives the authors the characteristics of the major players, as well as their history and the main story threads everyone will be working with. Everyone then understands the pace

at which the stories must unfold, which characters will be featured in each story, and what plot twists and turns must be present in each book in order to move the main story forward. The bible is distinct for every project, and provides descriptions of buildings, maps, etc., so that all the authors are working with common material. As authors begin to write their stories, adjustments sometimes need to be made. Those changes are cleared with the managing editor and communicated to the other authors, in order to avoid inconsistencies developing between the stories.

Who checks the facts for consistency?

6 One of the most complicated elements of a limited continuity is that, while the main story unfolds step-by-step in consecutive books, the stories are actually being written simultaneously. The authors are in constant communication with one another to ensure that their facts and story lines are consistent as each writer moves forward, infusing the individual stories with her own imagination and bringing it to life in her own distinctive way.

In order to ensure consistency, one editor edits all twelve books consecutively and is responsible for checking that the characterization of the continuing players does not change from book to book. The editor makes sure that the story lines follow logically, building to a climax and satisfying ending.

How long does this take?
There is usually a span of at least eighteen months
to two years between the time that a concept is first
proposed and when the first book of a continuing
series appears in your bookstore.

Look for a new FORTUNES OF TEXAS: REUNION
story every month at your favorite retailer.

The Writing Life

USA TODAY bestselling author Marie Ferrarella has written more than 150 books for Silhouette Books. Here's the inside scoop on how she comes up with ideas and develops her characters.

Everyone always asks, "Where do you get your ideas?" The simplest answer is, they come when I call them. When I'm lucky, something will just occur to me out of the blue when I'm going along (the old lightbulb-going-off-over-your-head syndrome). Very quickly, one incident knits itself into another and before you know it, you've got a bare bones skeleton begging for skin, for muscles, for hair color, nail polish, etc. Most of the time, however, it's a matter of my sitting down before that dreaded empty white screen and trying to come up with a viable idea for a story. You start with an idea. Follow: A guy comes back to attend the funeral of an old friend. Staying in his old room at home, he relives some of the feelings, the thoughts he had once when he was younger. He opens his closet, sees his old high school jacket and on a whim, puts it on. When he puts his hands into his pockets, he finds a letter from his ex-girlfriend in one of them. And off we go.

I find that I have just the barest of ideas, and as I begin to write, things happen. Magic. There's no better way to describe it than that. Friends, neighbors, quirks I never knew about my character suddenly come up as if they were there all along—except while I was writing the outline. The magic of a story is in the telling of a story, and the trick is to always keep an open mind. For instance, I needed to fill out a story I was working on. I happened to see a human-interest story about a woman who decided to begin a career in stand-up comedy when she was seventy. And just like that, an eccentric neighbor for my heroine was born.

Happily, I don't live in a vacuum (my dog would bark at me all the time). Life is going on all around me. I cannibalize everything I can if it'll make a better story because readers can identify with these common, everyday occurrences and it makes them more sympathetic to my hero or heroine. My first draft is always to have two people in a vacuum, naked, talking. With each pass, I add more until they're dressed, have attitudes and back stories. Then they move forward. As to any research that might be necessary, I do that as I go along, relying on the simplest paths to get my information. Readers don't want to read a definitive history about the development of the airplane, they just want to see my heroine fly the plane and then they want to move on with the story. And so do I. Because there's always another story waiting for me in the wings. Not bad for someone who only thought she had two stories in her.

Be sure to look for *The Best Medicine* by Marie Ferrarella, available from Signature Select in July 2005 and *Searching for Cate* by Marie Ferrarella, available from Signature Select in August 2005.

Here's a sneak peek...

IN THE ARMS
OF THE LAW

by
Peggy Moreland

You won't want to miss the continuation of THE FORTUNES OF TEXAS: REUNION, a new 12-book continuity series featuring the powerful Fortune family. Enjoy this excerpt of Peggy Moreland's In the Arms of the Law, the third book in the series—available August 2005.

SNEAK PEEK BONUS FEATURE

ONE

Andi Matthews was no stranger to murder. She'd focused her entire college career on studying the profiles of killers and perfecting the procedures for gathering the evidence needed to win convictions. For the past nine years she'd worked for the Red Rock Police Department, had personally investigated close to fifty murders and put nearly that same number of criminals behind bars. She knew how a murderer's mind worked, what fueled their need to kill and what mistakes they might make that would lead to their arrests.

But she'd never considered committing murder herself.

Until today.

From the moment Chief Prater had assigned Gabe Thunderhawk to work with her to identify the body of the Lost Fortune—the tag given to the floater discovered at Lake Mondo—she'd known she was in for trouble. Everyone on the force knew that Gabe wanted a promotion to detective, and this was the perfect chance for him to prove he was qualified to handle the job.

Intellectually she understood what a boon the successful closing of the case would be to his career. Because of the crown-shaped birthmark on the floater's right hip that linked the body with the Fortune family, solving the case would give him a level of publicity and notoriety that no other case could offer.

But understanding his motive in no way excused his behavior. Not in Andi's opinion. *She* was the primary on this case and she was sick and tired of him working independently from her. They were supposed to be partners, a team; she intended to remind him of that fact the moment he showed up…if he ever did.

She stopped her agitated pacing in front of the police station and shoved up the sleeve of her blazer to check the time. Her frown deepened as she noted that he was now over thirty minutes late.

"Okay, Thunderhawk," she muttered under her breath. "What are you up to now?"

While playing the possibilities through her mind, she recalled mentioning the day before that they should re-question the fishing guide who had found the body. Figuring Gabe had taken it upon himself to do the job alone—and upstaging her should he get lucky—she headed for her unmarked, city-issue Ford sedan.

The twenty-minute drive to Lake Mondo gave her ample time to work up a pretty good head of steam.

By the time she arrived at Hook 'n' Go, the bait shop where the fishing guide usually hung out, and found Gabe's truck parked out front, she was a slash mark beyond the boiling point. Prepared to read him the riot act for his traitorous behavior the moment he showed his double-crossing face, she braced a hip against the hood of his truck, folded her arms across her chest and waited.

Her timing was perfect, as moments later, the door of the bait shop opened and Gabe appeared. Seemingly unaware of her presence, he paused in the doorway, conversing with someone inside. He didn't appear rushed or harried, a fact that grated on her already raw nerves, since he'd kept her cooling her heels for almost an hour. But Gabe never seemed to get in a hurry, a trait the guys on the force attributed to his Native American heritage. That same heritage was evident by his high slash of cheekbones, the bronze tint of his skin, his dark hair and eyes. Most women considered him drop-dead handsome. Normally Andi would've agreed.

Today she considered him nothing but a royal pain in the ass.

"I appreciate your time," she heard him say to the person inside. "If you think of anything, you've got my card." The slap of the screen door closing was followed by the scrape of his boot soles on the worn wooden steps as he headed for his truck.

When he spotted Andi, he slowed slightly then strode on, his brow wrinkled in puzzlement.

"What are you doing here?" he asked. "I thought we were supposed to meet at the station."

"Oh, we were," she replied, then pushed away from his truck with a scowl, and leveled a warning finger at his nose. "Listen up, Thunderhawk, and listen good. Whether you like it or not, I'm the primary on this investigation, and nothing is done outside of my presence or without my prior knowledge, including interviewing individuals associated with this case."

He held up a hand. "Now wait a minute. You're the one who said we should talk to the fishing guide again."

"Yes, I did. But *we* didn't talk to him, *you* did, and after being told repeatedly that we work as a team." She narrowed an eye. "I'm warning you, Gabe, if you continue to undermine my authority, I'll request that Chief Prater remove you from the case."

He hitched his hands on his hips in frustration. "What is it with you, anyway? You act like I'm sneaking around behind your back."

"Well, aren't you?"

"What I was trying to do was save us both some time."

"And how did you plan to do that, when I've been sitting on my hands at the station for over an hour waiting for you?"

"My place is a couple of miles from here. I figured I'd stop by on my way into town, question the guide then meet you at the station and report my findings. Is it my fault the fishing guide is a Chatty Cathy?"

Though his explanation made sense, she didn't trust him. Not for minute. This wasn't the first time he'd struck out on his own without first discussing his plans with her. But to continue to debate his insubordination would be unproductive and a waste of more of her time.

She released a breath and, along with it, some of her anger. "All right," she said, grudgingly. "But next time check with me first or I swear I'll file a complaint with the chief."

"Fine."

Determined to focus her mind on the investigation and away from her irritation with her so-called partner, she asked, "Did the guide have anything new to say?"

He lifted a shoulder. "Same story he gave the day he found the body."

She hadn't expected the man would remember anything new. But after two months with no new leads on the case, there was nothing left to do but backtrack, in hope of finding something they'd missed the first time through.

Frustrated by the lack of evidence they had to work with, she frowned at the lake that had regurgitated the Lost Fortune, washing its bloated body up on shore. Thanks to the southeasterly wind currently blowing, the lake's surface was choppy. Not a fishing or pleasure boat in sight. A lone heron sailed low over the water, trolling for his next meal. The shore-line itself was empty of humanity, but dotted with lit-ter: aluminum cans, plastic bags and a length of frayed synthetic rope, probably discarded from some ski boat. It was a scavenger's dream.

As she watched a wave wash the litter higher onto shore, an idea began to grow in her mind.

"What was the weather like the day before the body was discovered?"

He gave her an impatient look. "How the hell would I know?"

"If we can find out which direction the wind was blowing prior to the body being found, we might be able to pinpoint the area where it was dumped."

"Yeah," he said dryly, "and if we had a crystal ball we could probably look inside and see who dumped it."

She burned him with a look. "Do you have a bet-ter idea?"

He turned and walked away.

"Where are you going?" she asked in frustration.

"Inside," he called over his shoulder. "Ten-to-one the owner of the bait shop keeps a weather journal."

Kicking herself for not having thought of that her-self, she watched Gabe walk toward the bait shop. She wished she'd kept her eyes on the lake as seeing his backside reminded her of the notice she'd seen on the bulletin board in the women's restroom that morning. A bright yellow banner announcing that the female employees had awarded Gabe the "Cutest

Butt on the Force" award. She let her gaze slide to his hips. Even though she thought the awards were stupid, she had to agree. He did have a fine-looking tush.

Unfortunately, his butt wasn't his only outstanding feature. Wide shoulders; slim waist; muscled chest, arms and legs. He was the only man she knew who could make a department-issue khaki uniform look as if it was custom-tailored for him by Armani.

Too bad he'd let his physical attributes go to his head. He had an ego the size of Texas and was a playboy to boot. Two traits that, in her mind at least, nullified his finer points.

With a sigh, she turned her gaze to the lake and waited. To pass the time she counted the waves that rushed onto shore.

"Wind was from the northwest," Gabe reported moments later as he rejoined her. "Gusts up to seventy-two miles per hour."

She glanced at the sun, seeking a point of reference, then across the span of white-capped water toward the northwest quadrant of the lake. "Do you know what's over there?"

"A few private homes, a public boat ramp and acres of undeveloped land."

"I say we start with the public ramp," she said and turned for her car.

He fell into step beside her. "We can take my truck."

"No way. I value my life too much to climb into a vehicle with you behind the wheel."

"Hey," he said, sounding insulted. "There's nothing wrong with my driving." He stopped at the side of his truck and opened the passenger door. "Besides, my truck's got four-wheel drive. Depending on how far you want to explore, we might need it."

She hesitated a moment, considering, then heaved a sigh and climbed inside, knowing he was right.

"No speeding," she warned as he slid behind the wheel. "And none of those fancy one-eighties they teach at the police academy."

He put the truck in gear, shot her a grin then spun the wheel and stomped on the accelerator. With a squeal of tires, they were headed in the opposite direction. Andi grabbed for the chicken bar above the passenger window and hung on, silently vowing to kill him later.

By the time they reached the turnoff for the boat ramp, her knuckles were white and her feet burned from pressing on the imaginary brake on the floorboard on her side of the vehicle. Thankfully, the road that led to the ramp was full of potholes, which forced him to slow down. It was also bordered by shoulder-high weeds and even taller cedars, the perfect cover for someone who had something—or someone—to hide. As they neared the lake, the road widened, with parking space available to the left and the right of a long, weathered dock.

As soon as he pulled to a stop, Andi opened her

20

door and jumped to the ground. "Next time I drive," she muttered irritably.

Gabe met her at the hood. "You shouldn't have said anything about my driving. It was like a dare." He lifted a brow and looked down his nose at her. "And I've never been able to walk away from a dare."

"I'll remember that in the future," she said dryly, then pushed up her sleeves, eager to get to work. "Okay. Here's how we're going to play this. We'll assume that the murder took place somewhere other than at the lake."

"Any particular reason?"

"Mainly because none of the residents who live around the lake reported hearing gunshots."

"He could have used a silencer."

"True, but my gut tells me the murder took place somewhere else and the killer used the lake as a depository, hoping the body would never be discovered."

He lifted a shoulder. "You're the boss."

"We're also going to assume that the murderer dumped the body at night. Otherwise, he'd risk being seen."

"I can buy that," he agreed.

She stepped to the edge of the water and frowned as she studied the moss-covered concrete ramp that stretched beyond the surface. "So what would he do?" she asked, thinking aloud, as she tried to slip into the mind of the murderer. "Back his vehicle to the edge, as if he was going to put a boat into the water, then dump the body?" She cut her gaze to the pier. "Or would he carry it onto the dock and drop it over the side?"

"Depends on his physical condition. If our perp is in good shape, he'd probably carry the body to the end of the dock. The water's deeper there. It would also save him from getting wet."

She nodded her agreement.

"There's also the possibility that he used a boat," he reminded her. "He could have concealed the body in the hull prior to driving to the lake, put in here at the ramp then shoved the body overboard once he was far enough away from the shoreline to avoid detection."

22

"Yes, but we've already checked with the owners of the boats known to be on the water that night. Each was aware of the others' presence and all agreed that theirs were the only boats on the lake. All three owners were questioned individually and their stories matched."

"Then we go with the theory that the murderer dumped the body from the dock or shore."

"For now." She turned away. "You check the shoreline. I'll take the dock."

"Wait a minute," he said, stopping her. "Any evidence left behind would've washed away or been destroyed by now."

"Maybe we'll get lucky."

Though she could tell by his expression that he considered the search a waste of time, he didn't offer anymore arguments. Surprised that he was cooperating with her for a change, she continued on for the dock.

As she stepped onto the weathered surface, the barrels that supported it pitched beneath her weight. She gave herself a moment to adjust to the rolling movement, then walked slowly to the opposite end, casting her gaze from side to side. Long strands of slimy-looking vegetation swayed beneath the surface of the murky water, tugged by the current. She stifled a shudder. She loved swimming, but preferred man-made pools with concrete bottoms and chlorine-treated water over lakes, with all their aquatic vegetation and muddy base.

At the end of the dock, she squatted down and looked over the edge, trying to imagine the murderer's movements if he'd chosen this particular method to dispose of the body. Several feet beneath the water's surface, she caught a glimpse of a scrap of fabric snagged on one of the support posts.

Though she knew the chances of the fabric being torn from the Lost Fortune's clothing were slim, she pushed up a sleeve and reached to retrieve it. Just short of touching the water, she jerked her hand back to fist against her thigh. She gulped as she stared into the murky water. She wasn't a sissy. Not by any stretch of the imagination. But she had a deathly fear of snakes, and water moccasins, one of Texas's most poisonous snakes, made their homes in lakes and ponds.

Catching her lower lip between her teeth, she glanced Gabe's way, thinking she'd ask him to retrieve the piece of cloth.

But if she did, she would be exposing her fear of snakes, something she was reluctant to do, as she knew she would be setting herself up to be on the receiving end of practical jokes from not only Gabe, but every guy on the force. Rubber snakes in her desk. Curled on the seat of her car. Stuffed into her mail slot. The possibilities were endless.

With a sigh of resignation, she shrugged off her blazer, leaving her arms bare, then drew in a deep breath and thrust her hand into the water. She shuddered in revulsion as long strands of weeds brushed against her fingers and wound around her arm. The colorful bit of fabric swayed inches from her fingertips, and she leaned farther over, straining to reach it.

"Just a little bit more," she encouraged under her breath.

She heard a sharp popping sound and, at the same moment, felt the plank beneath her right knee give way. She only had time to draw in one shocked breath before the board broke and she was pitched headfirst into the water.

As she plunged downward, vegetation grabbed at her and slapped at her face. In her mind, each tendril was a snake, slithering over her skin. She wanted to scream, but the thought of swallowing even a teaspoon of the vile water kept the sound lodged in her throat.

Fear had her kicking hard and fighting her way back to the top. As she broke through the surface, she released the scream that burned in her throat. Sobbing, she clawed at the slime that clung to her arms and chest while trying to remain afloat.

Something hard and flat slammed against the top of her head—a pressure she realized was Gabe's hand a split second before he shoved her down under the water. She came up sputtering and slapping at him, blinded by the water in her eyes.

"Andi!" he shouted. "Relax! I've got you."

Before she could tell him she wasn't drowning, he hooked an arm beneath her chin and began to drag her toward shore. Once on the bank, he released her, dumping her unceremoniously in the mud and moss on the concrete boat ramp.

He dropped down next to her and blew out a long breath. "Lucky thing I was here," he said. "Otherwise you might've drowned."

Sprawled in mud and slime, she pushed up to her elbows and scowled at his back. "I wasn't drowning, you idiot."

He glanced over his shoulder. "Then why the scream?"

Embarrassed that he'd heard that, she sat up and brushed at the weeds that clung to her slacks, avoiding his gaze. "I'm scared of snakes," she admitted reluctantly.

He stared a moment, then hooted a laugh. "Hell, if there was a snake within a mile of you, you would've scared it away with all that flapping around you were doing." He pushed to his feet. "We better get out of these wet clothes." He offered her a hand. "Come on. Let's go to my place and get cleaned up. I've got a washer and dryer."

Though she'd have preferred a long soak in her own tub, the thought of the thirty-odd-minute drive back to town in muddy clothes made her reconsider. "All right," she agreed and allowed him to pull her to her feet. "But I'm getting that piece of fabric off the post before I go anywhere."

"I'll get it."

She knew she should insist upon retrieving it herself, to prove to him she wasn't a coward. But the thought of going anywhere near that pier kept her lips sealed tight.

She watched him drop down on his stomach at the end of the pier and reach into the water. "Can you tell what it is?" she called as he pulled his arm out.

He stood and lifted the scrap of fabric for her to see. "Orange canvas from a life preserver. Judging by its rotted state, I'd say it's been here for years."

Her shoulders sagged in disappointment.

Another dead end.

...NOT THE END...

Look for In the Arms of the Law *by Peggy Moreland in stores August 2005.*